# THE NANNY

*A BWWM Billionaire Romance*

## IMANI KING

"Y ou should apply!" Samantha said from over her shoulder, nearly making Trisha jump out of her skin. After taking a few deep breaths to keep her heart from leaping from her chest and bolting for the door, Trisha turned and glared at her.

"Privacy much?"

She didn't even blink at the rebuff. "Looking for young, energetic person able to keep up with two growing boys. Full-time salary with benefits? Yes please! And look… it's a couple blocks off campus! You'd be *perfect* for it."

"Yeah, along with the five thousand other people who would apply." Trisha closed the webpage, then shut her laptop. The listing had come up when she was scrolling through Facebook, killing time before heading to class. The job looked nice, but if it *looked* too good to be true, it probably was.

"But you love kids! You've been babysitting since you were thirteen. You're majoring in child psychology! Hell, I'm surprised you're not married with kids of your own by now." Samantha crossed her arms and stared me down, apparently not willing to let this go without a fight. "You should apply. What's the worst that'll happen?"

"And waste time I could be spending on my studies?" I said, sarcasm dripping from my voice. "Besides, this is a full-time job, not a babysitting gig. It's completely different."

Trisha did love kids. It was one of the reasons she was a psych major. Ever since she was in high school she'd wanted to become a child psychiatrist or a social worker. Sure, they weren't *high paying* jobs and it would be stressful work, but she didn't really see herself doing anything else.

Playing full-time nanny for some wealthy jerk wasn't even on the radar… and besides, she'd never fit into that kind of life.

Trisha had been lucky to grow up in a lower middle

class family. They didn't have much, but there were few things she'd *wanted* for growing up. Her parents had both worked full-time to support the family and they gave her a chance to choose her own future… even if she'd need to take out some student loans to pay for it.

She wanted to help the kids who weren't so lucky.

Samantha frowned, but dropped the subject, at least for now. Trisha already knew this wouldn't be the last she heard of it. Once Sam had her mind set on something, she was like a rabid dog that wouldn't let go. All Trisha could hope for was that the position would fill up quickly and Sam would be forced to move on to some other silly obsession.

Sam flopped down on the couch and watched Trisha as she crammed her things into her bag. Unlike Trisha, Sam's first class started at noon. She'd thought she was lucky getting a 9am class as her first one of the day, but part of her wished she'd followed Sam's example instead. At least the campus was only a short walk from here. She didn't have to worry about a long commute or traffic, so she didn't have to get up as early as some of the students did.

Besides, Trisha was a junior now and used to getting up fairly early.

"You should at least *think* about that job!" Samantha yelled as Trisha headed for the door. "You *already* had to cut back on classes."

"It's not my fault they raised tuition again…"

"And that means you've got the time! Besides, if you don't do this you're just gonna end up waitressing again."

"I am NOT waitressing again!" Trisha shouted. Waffle House helped pay for her first year of college, but it was an experience she wouldn't wish on her worst enemy. Some of her shoes *still* smelled like syrup…

"Says the girl who just filled out an Applebees application," Samantha said, laughing.

Sam was right, of course. She usually was. Trisha's scholarship didn't come close to covering tuition, let alone room and board. She couldn't call her parents for help, and that meant the loans were already piling up. A full-time job with a full-time income would go a *long* way toward fixing things, even if it only lasted a semester or two.

"Good bye, Samantha," Trisha said, biting her tongue, "and stop snooping around in my stuff!"

"Don't forget! Taco Tuesday with the guys at seven!" she shouted as Trisha closed the door.

Yeah, like she was going to forget that. It was the one day a week she got out of the apartment. If it wasn't for Sam, and Brandon, and Justin, she'd have been a social pariah, burying herself in textbooks and school work.

*I could at least apply for the job…*

A job would be another great way to get out of the house. Hell, even if she spent most of her time taking care of kids, it'd be better than staring at her laptop all night. Maybe she could even talk this guy into being a job reference once she had her degree…

Trisha was so caught up in her own thoughts, her body walking on auto-pilot, that she hadn't noticed the man until she walked dead into him. He shouted as his coffee jostled, splattering all over the front of his suit jacket.

"Oh my god!" Trisha gasped in horror. She reached into her purse and rummaged around until she found a napkin and immediately began to try and wipe it up.

The man growled and snatched the cloth from her to clean himself up. Trisha stood rooted in place as she stared at the unexpected *distraction* of a man. He was gorgeous in the way no living person deserved to be. Tall, of course, with dark brown hair cropped just long enough to run your fingers through. His chiseled features may as well have been carved from marble, and the expensive suit was perfectly tailored to his muscular body. That would have been enough to drool over, but he topped it off with emerald green eyes that blazed hot enough to burn right through you.

Her mouth was moving, but no words were coming out.

He didn't seem to be struck with the same affliction.

"You should watch where you're going," he said, his voice deep enough to make her heart skip a beat.

Trisha nodded rapidly, her brain bouncing around in her head. "Yes, yes! I'm sorry, so sorry." Trisha rambled on, desperate to apologize for bumping into this man.

The man frowned at his coffee-stained jacket, then let out a sigh. Trisha swallowed as she followed his gaze, watching dollar signs appearing before her eyes. If he was going to ask her to pay for it, there was no way she could afford it. She couldn't even afford to *dry clean* a suit like that!

"Be more careful, please," he said before handing back the wet napkin. She didn't get another word out as he brushed past her and continued down the sidewalk.

Trisha was rooted to the spot as she watched him go, letting out a little sigh of relief. *Well, that could've been worse*, she thought to herself. That was a hell of a way to start her morning. Trisha prayed she wouldn't run into him again, then turned and headed toward campus.

C ould this day get any worse? Jonathan wondered as he pushed the office doors open. Everyone greeted him with a wave or a smile, and he nodded at them, eager to lock himself in the office for a few hours. Peace and quiet were just what the doctor ordered after a morning like this.

Declan had thrown a fit again, insisting he wasn't going to school today. It'd taken both him *and* Alexander to get the boy into his uniform, and he'd pouted the whole way to school. It'd been like this ever since Grace decided to retire. Jonathan had pleaded with her to stay on, but she'd been the family nanny since *he* was young enough to need one.

She deserved her retirement, and he couldn't really argue with that.

But he *also* thought he could make it more than two weeks without going insane.

That was proving to be a challenge. He'd spent the last couple days running around like a crazed animal. Picking up the kids, dropping them off, trying desperately to keep the house from falling apart. In just forty-eight hours he'd discovered a whole new respect for Grace and everything she'd done for him over the years… like the way she was always keeping legos off the floor. It doesn't seem like much of a big deal until one of those little plastic bastards try to kill you. The arch of his foot was *still* aching.

There was no time to sit around lamenting his tragic lego injury, of course. Traffic had been a bitch, which just put him even further behind schedule… and when he'd limped down to the coffee shop to grab himself something to drink, some pretty little college girl dumped a caramel macchiato straight down his jacket.

He barely even acknowledged Carla, his personal secretary, before stepping into his corner office. He tossed the empty cup into the garbage, then flopped down onto the soft couch and closed his eyes. This was the kind of day where crawling under some blankets and refusing to come out might have been an acceptable coping strategy. It'd beat working, at any rate.

Of course… as hard as things were, he'd be lying if he wasn't loving every minute of it. He'd spent more time with his kids in the last two days than he had over the last two *months*. Running a Fortune 500 company required sacrifice, and coming home after his boys were already in bed was one of the hardest things in the world to do.

Hell, maybe he'd leave work early tonight. The three of them could relax in the theater and have a movie night.

At that moment, a mindless action flick sounded pretty good… and it would be nice to spend a *little* more time with the kids before he found a new nanny and got his life back on the rails.

A knocking on the door sent him back to the real world. Jonathan stood back up and removed the stained jacket, leaving in on the armrest as he walked over to his desk. "Come in," he said as he sat down, frowning at the papers already stacked up in front of him.

"Rough morning?" Carla asked as she walked in.

Jonathan snorted. "That's an understatement."

Carla must've read his mind, because she was already working on solutions. "We've had a lot of applicants for the nanny position. I was thinking of having the best candidates come in for an interview with you. Does that sound okay?"

"It sounds great," he said with a nod. "I also want the boys to meet anyone I'm thinking of hiring. I don't want them stuck with someone they hate."

"Perfect!" Carla grinned, then set more papers on the desk. "These just came up from accounting. They need your approval."

He sighed and flipped through them. He absolutely loved the job, but dear God did he despise the paperwork. Was there any sane person who enjoyed watching numbers shuffle their way across a spreadsheet?

He doubted it.

"I'll get to these right away." Jonathan smiled up at her. "I don't know what I'd have done without you these past few weeks. You've been a lifesaver, and I really appreciate your help with the nanny search."

"It's my pleasure." She winked at him. "Just remember how impressed you are when my Christmas bonus goes out this year!" With a laugh, she headed toward the door. "Buzz me if you need anything."

Jonathan shook his head. Carla never was one to beat

around the bush! "Don't worry, I won't forget! And try not to work yourself too hard out there."

Once Carla was gone, he let out a sigh and leaned back in his chair, closing his eyes again. This was going to be a long day and an even longer week. With a little luck he'd have a nanny in place before it was over.

After a few moments of deep breathing, Jonathan sat up and looked at the stack of paperwork. It wasn't getting any smaller, so he grabbed the first page and got to work.

## 3

### TRISHA

School seemed to drag on forever. Even though she actually liked the class, her professor should've retired eons ago. The material was fascinating, but his heart clearly wasn't in it. He droned on, doing the absolute minimum required to maintain his tenure. Watching paint dry might have been more interesting.

But that only allowed her mind to drift.

More than once during the day, she thought about that nanny job. Should she take Sam's advice and apply for the job? Depending on how old the kids were, it wouldn't be too bad. If they were in school she'd have half the day to finish up her own classes.

It was sounding better and better every time she ran over it. By the time she finally met Sam and the guys at the local tacoria, the job was still sitting at the front of her mind. She tried to focus on dinner instead.

"Did you see they came out with new coke zero?" Brandon asked, grinning at the three of us. "They say it tastes better…"

Trisha groaned and shook her head. Brandon's obsession with all things soda-related during their game nights bordered on unhealthy. "I swear I'm going to find out you have a Coca-Cola body pillow one of these days." Trisha stuck her tongue out at him, then took a bite of her taco.

"That sounds like something a Pepsi drinker would say!" Brandon stuck his nose up in the air, making everyone laugh.

*I wish I could do this more than once a week*, Trish thought to herself. But with her current budget, even once a week was pushing it. Pretty soon, she was going to have to start choosing between school or *food*…

As everyone chatted and joked some more, Trisha made up her mind. She would apply for the nanny position when she got home. The job was well within her skills, and the extra money would be fantastic. Hell… she might even end up with some savings at the end of this.

A grin etched onto her face, she let everyone keep on talking and pulled out her iPhone.

The grin didn't last long. As soon as the job listing page loaded, the word CLOSED appeared in big letters over top.

Fuck!

She cursed herself mentally. Samantha was right: It'd been the perfect job. Why hadn't she just applied for it this morning when Sam told her to?

Still frowning, Trisha excused herself from the little social gathering. Brandon had moved onto arguing about whether or not aspartame gives you cancer, and Sam looked pretty busy chatting up a cute guy up by the tequila bar. They'd barely even notice she was gone…

Which was probably for the best. She didn't really want to explain her sudden change in mood.

Trisha made it home and grabbed a shower before crawling beneath her fluffy blanket. Sleep was fitful that night. When her alarm went off that morning, she already knew it was going to be a two-pots-of-coffee kind of day. Sam was still sound asleep, thankfully, so at least Trisha didn't have to listen to an "I told you so!" over the job.

She was halfway through her second class of the day when her phone started buzzing in her pocket. When she pulled it out, an unknown local number flashed across the screen. She thought about ignoring it, but a nagging feeling told her not to. As quietly as possible, she crept out of the classroom. Once the door shut behind her, she answered the call.

"Hello?"

"Hello!" the cheery voice on the other end replied. "Is this Miss Holcut?"

"The one and only," Trish replied, leaning against the cool brick wall. Nobody called her Miss Holcut except her mother and half a dozen bill collectors… and her mother never sounded this happy in her life.

"Great! We wanted to see if you could come in today for an interview."

"An interview?"

"For the nanny position you applied for." The woman's voice held steady, its sing-song tones pouring over the line. Trisha could almost *hear* her smiling. "You sent in the application yesterday morning."

Now Trisha was confused. Sure, she'd looked at the listing yesterday, but it was closed before she could apply.

*Samantha.*

The little witch had gone behind Trisha's back and applied for her! Trisha told her she wasn't interested!

She couldn't be mad about it… she *had* wanted to apply for the job, even if it took her awhile to make up her mind. It certainly explained why Sam hadn't mentioned anything about the job last night.

"Yes, excellent. When would you like me to come interview?"

"Are you free this afternoon?"

"Sure! Absolutely!"

Trish took deep breaths, trying to calm her nerves. The last thing she wanted was to seem too eager.

"Perfect. Can you come in around two?"

Trisha finalized the meeting with the woman on the phone and even managed to wait until they'd hung up before jumping up and down. She owed Samantha a hug and a smack upside the head when she saw her later.

Sam was still in class when Trisha went back to the apartment to change. She must've gone through a dozen outfits before she settled on one she liked. What *were* you supposed to wear to interview for a nanny job?

She finally settled on a black blouse and a mid-length black skirt to match. It was normally an outfit she reserved for events that warranted a professional look and was *probably* the fanciest thing she owned…

*If I get this job, the first thing I'm doing is going clothes shopping…* Trish thought as she walked to the office the woman had directed her to. Thankfully, it wasn't far from her apartment. By the time she sat down in the reception area, her heart had begun thundering. What if she wasn't dressed nice enough? What if they wanted someone with more experience?

An endless stream of doubt flashed through her mind until the secretary's phone rang. When she set the receiver down, she grinned widely at Trisha.

"Mr. Ashcourt is ready for you."

She stood and opened the office door. The moment Trisha was inside, the door shut behind her, making her jump slightly. She took a deep breath, then crossed the small room to the desk at the other end, freezing in place as she made eye contact with the man behind it.

Fucking hell.

Of all the ways she could have screwed up this inter-view, this had to take the cake. Staring her down was Mr. Sexy-as-hell himself… minus one coffee stained jacket.

## 4

# JONATHAN

J onathan smiled up at the woman, waving toward one of the seats. "Please, sit."

Whatever confidence she seemed to have when she walked in had all but evaporated. He watched as she nodded and moved on shaking legs to sit in front of him, taking a moment to glance up to her unforgettable eyes.

"Thank you for coming in on such short notice, Miss Holcut."

"Trisha, please!" The woman squeaked out.

Jonathan smiled at her, trying to put her at ease. "Trisha then. Are you here to ruin another suit?"

"That's... I... I..."

23

"I'm sorry, I couldn't help myself," Jonathan laughed. "Don't worry, I managed to get the stain out."

"Should I… go?" Trisha asked quietly.

"Seems like that'd be a waste of a job interview, don't you think? I loved reading over your application. It was quite… *creative*. Tell me Trisha… have you ever been a nanny before?"

She shook her head, a look of worry flashing across her face. "I babysat through middle and high school. I've never had a formal nanny position, but I work with kids all the time. I interned with the Family Crisis Center and helped run an early education program with Montgomery Elementary…"

He'd known that from her resume, of course. Babysitting experience would be helpful when chasing around the boys, and her experience in an educational environment would be great when the kids brought home schoolwork to finish. He also particularly liked her college emphasis in child psychology. She wasn't a fully qualified psychologist, but she knew more than the average nanny might…

That might come in handy when dealing with Declan, and it put her a step above several of the other nannies he'd interviewed. Besides that, his gut was telling him to hire her. If this had been a job at his company, that alone would have been enough to pull the trigger… but he needed to be a bit more *thorough* when his children were involved.

"Tell me about your hobbies," Jonathan said.

Trisha blinked at him, the question seeming to surprise her. She thought about it for a moment before responding. "Nothing exciting. I spend most of my free time reading and studying. I'm trying to maintain my 4.0 average."

"Well, the boys could certainly learn a thing or two about good study habits," he grinned at her and Trisha smiled back. "Will you have time for this job with your school schedule? I'm offering a *generous* salary, but my expectations are very high. I require more than a babysitter. You'll be a full time live-in nanny, and as one of the many benefits, I will be providing you free room and board for the duration of your work contract. I will provide you with a large guest suite, and you'll be responsible for getting my two boys off to school and for picking them up every day. You will be taking care of all after-school activities up to and including bed-time, and I'll be expecting you to *enrich* my children's lives… not to *watch* them."

Jonathan sighed and leaned back in his chair. "It's not an easy job. I'm always stuck at the office well past dinnertime. On the days I'm not, I'm probably on a red-eye flight taking care of business out-of-state. I'll need you to care for the children when I'm traveling for a few days at a time. You won't have to worry about cooking or cleaning. I've hired someone to take care of that for the time being. You'd be purely responsible for the kids, but if you get settled in, we can discuss promoting you to a larger role in the household."

"A larger role?" Trisha asked.

"My former nanny handled *all* household duties… and I can assure you she was incredibly well compensated for her efforts."

Trisha seemed a little taken aback by all of this. "So… you're asking me to move in with you?"

"You might be getting a little ahead of yourself Trisha. I haven't offered you the job yet," Jonathan replied, grinning wide.

"My college classes won't be a problem. I'm not taking a full load this semester, and I can schedule them during school hours which gives me plenty of time to drop off and pick up the children. I can finish up any extra projects or coursework after they've gone to bed."

Jonathan nodded. That seemed reasonable.

She wasn't as qualified as the other two nannies he'd already interviewed, but she *was* unique. The others had been older than he was, and after dealing with one retirement he wasn't ready for another. He'd gotten lucky with Grace, since she'd been there for the boys since they were babies... but now that they were growing up, it seemed like he should hire someone who could stick around a little longer.

He knew Trisha probably had bigger plans for the future. She would finish college and expect to go into her field of study. That was, of course, a problem *money* could solve. He could offer her a salary that would outpace anything available in the world of psychology. When the time came, he was confident he could keep her around... if the children liked her.

"Would you mind coming to the house for dinner tonight?" Jonathan flinched. That sounded like he was propositioning her! Hastily, he added "I'd like you to meet the boys and see how they react before I make any hiring decisions."

Trisha nodded, grinning at him. "*That* would be fine! I've got some homework to catch up on, but it won't be an issue."

Jonathan stood and extended his hand. Trisha stood almost instantly clasping hands with him. "It's settled then. I'll send a car to come pick you up."

"Try not to spill any coffee on your way out," he added with a smirk and a wink.

Trisha practically ran from the room. Jonathan chuckled as the door shut behind her, then dropped back into his chair.

Even with her gone, he could still see those deep brown eyes in his mind. With a sigh, he pushed those thoughts away. She was stunningly beautiful in every single way, but he was looking for a nanny... not a date.

❧ 5 ❧

## TRISHA

**T**risha skipped on her way back to the apartment. She couldn't believe she was actually getting a shot at the job. There had to have been more qualified applicants for a job like this, especially in a city the size of Atlanta. She wondered if he'd invited anyone else to dinner…

That would make things uncomfortable.

The moment she was in the apartment, she ran to her room and began tearing her wardrobe apart. This outfit had been good for an interview, but she needed something a bit more… personal. She wanted the boys to like her, and if she looked like she was dressing for a funeral, that might not happen.

It took almost an hour, but she finally settled on a light business casual outfit with pastel colors. It would be formal enough that Mr. Ashcourt wouldn't toss her out, but casual enough that it would make her seem inviting to the kids.

As she stood in front of the mirror, she froze. She didn't even know how old the kids were, or their names. They could be anything from pre-schoolers to high schoolers! Fuck, fuck, fuck. Why hadn't she thought to ask while she was in the interview? She'd been so shocked to see him again that her brain had gone haywire.

She held the outfit up to her body and looked at it in the mirror again before tossing the top aside and choosing another. This one would be a little more conservative. The last thing she wanted was for Mr. Ashcourt to think she was trying to flash her breasts at him to get the job.

She wasn't going to be *that* kind of nanny…

She was still fretting when Sam came back from her last class. Storming out of the room, she found Sam standing in the foyer, flipping through her mail. Sam looked up in surprise when Trisha walked in.

"Something you want to tell me?" Trisha put her hands on her hips and glared at Sam. "I got a phone call today."

Sam was smart enough to look abashed as Trisha stared her down.

"They called me today while I was in class."

Sam's face lit up and she practically started bouncing up and down. "And? What'd they say? Come on, Trisha, you've gotta tell me!"

Trisha couldn't hold back her smile any more. She beamed at Sam and joined her in the bouncing excitement. "I had an interview after class! He wants me to come to dinner tonight and meet the kids. I think he's going to hire me…"

"Oh my god, that's amazing!" Sam threw herself at Trisha, hugging the bigger girl tight. Trisha wrapped her arms around Sam's waist, lifted her into the air, and spun her around until Sam squealed.

She never could stay mad at Sam for very long. They'd been best friends for longer than she could remember.

"I can't believe you sent in an application for me. I tried to apply after dinner, but the listing was closed. I thought I'd missed out on it."

Sam smirked, her head cocked slightly. This was what Trisha had been dreading; the 'I told you so' look that

Sam had perfected over the years. "Do I even need to say it?"

"Go ahead." Trisha sighed and rolled her eyes. She'd known it was coming the moment she'd gotten off the phone this morning. Might as well get it over with now.

"I told you so!" Sam stuck her tongue, then hugged Trisha. "You're going to get the job; I just know it."

The two celebrated a bit longer, then Trisha went to get ready. She spent extra time on her make-up and even had Sam braid her curly hair to help keep it in check. She wanted to make a good *third* impression…

She really wanted this job, even if she'd been hesitant before.

When her phone rang, her heart began to thunder again. Over and over she told herself she could do this. Now if only she could make herself believe it.

## 6

### JONATHAN

"You two be on your best behavior." He stared at both boys, locking eyes until they looked away. "Nothing is decided yet, so if you don't like her, I can keep searching, okay?"

Both of them nodded, but they didn't look very happy about any of this. "Why do we even need a babysitter? We're not babies anymore!" Declan said, looking up at his father and pouting.

"We can take care of ourselves," Alexander added. He crossed his arms in front of his chest. Jonathan had expected a bit of push-back from him. He was twelve but it was clear he saw himself as much too old to need someone to watch over him.

"First of all, she'd be your nanny, not your babysitter, just like Miss Grace. And I know you're not babies anymore, but you're still not old enough to be on your own, especially if I'm traveling."

The boys grumbled, but marched off toward the game room without much more complaint. Jonathan sighed, shaking his head as he watched them leave.

He hated having to replace Grace, but he didn't have much of a choice. He couldn't raise two growing boys and run a company without some help. He was already getting behind in his work, and he needed to get back on schedule soon. They had major projects going on at work, the kind that would determine the future of the company. This was probably the worst time for Grace to retire, but wasn't that just his luck? When it rains, it pours….

Jonathan was looking over some things on his laptop when the doorbell chimed, signaling the arrival of his guest. When he opened the door, Trisha was standing there looking slightly dazed, her dark eyes darting all over the place.

He stepped aside. "Please, come in," he said, waving his arm toward the foyer.

Trisha nodded and stepped in, still looking like a fish

out of water. He took a moment to run his eyes up and down her body. She'd changed into a new outfit, choosing a deep purple blouse and a pair of black slacks that showed off her assets. She definitely had a sense of style. Another positive in his book!

Once again, Jonathan chastised himself. She wasn't here for him. This was a business dinner and nothing more. *Strictly* business.

"Do you like the place?" he asked, desperate for conversation to help get his mind out of the gutter. Talking about anything would help get him back on track, he hoped.

Trisha nodded enthusiastically. "It's gorgeous! I've never been inside a house like this."

"I'm glad you like it." He led her into the sitting room. "Dinner should be ready soon. Can I get you a glass of wine?"

When Trisha nodded, he excused himself to the kitchen. Dinner smelled heavenly and made his stomach grumble as he poured the glasses. When he returned to the sitting room, he found Trisha standing by the bookshelves, her eyes running over each title.

"You said you enjoy reading," he said, handing her a glass.

"My mother used to read to me all the time when I was little. It was my favorite past-time growing up. The lady at the library near my house knew me on sight and would always put aside books she thought I might enjoy." She smiled fondly at the memory. "I used to love babysitting because it gave me plenty of time to read after the kids went to bed. The parents were always surprised when they'd come home and find me with my nose in a book instead of watching television."

Jonathan chuckled. As she spoke, he was more sure of his decision to choose her over the other candidates. He hoped her enthusiasm for books might rub off on the boys. God knew they could use less time in front of a screen and more time lost in a book! Then again, he wasn't going to get his hopes up. He'd need a miracle, not a nanny, to drag them away from their games.

"Would you like to meet the boys before we eat?" Jonathan asked. "They're in the game room right now, no doubt blowing things up again."

Trish smiled and nodded. "I'd love to."

Just as he'd expected, Declan and Alexander were on

the couch, their clothes wrinkled as they played some shooter game. Jonathan had given up trying to keep track of all the different games the boys played beyond checking the age recommendations.

"Boys, I'd like to introduce you to Miss Holcut."

Surprisingly, they paused the game and came over to greet her without me having to ask them twice. He took that as good sign.

"It's nice to meet you, Miss Holcut," they chorused at once.

"It's nice to meet you, too."

The boys began talking animatedly with Trisha. Jonathan gave up trying to follow the conversation and just watched them with a grin on his face. Alexander and Declan's apprehension about a new nanny seemed to vanish as they talked about everything from school lunch to video games with her.

By the time the four of them headed to dinner, it seemed like she'd won them over. They talked to her like she was an old friend. To her credit, she kept trying to drag Jonathan into the conversation, but it never took long before he was lost.

"So Trisha, how much longer are you in school?" Jonathan asked during a lull in the conversation.

"Another year and a half until I finish my Bachelor's degree. Then I'm going to apply to go for my Master's, if I can."

"Do you know where you'd like to study?"

She nodded. "Rand University. They have a fantastic graduate psychology program there."

The two talked a bit more about Trisha's plan for the future. He liked that she seemed to have a goal in mind and wasn't just drifting through life, trying to figure things out. For someone still fairly young, she was very grounded in reality. He also liked that she planned to stay local after she finished her Bachelor's. That meant it shouldn't be too difficult to keep working for him.

By the time dinner was over and the boys had run off to do god knows what, he'd made up his mind. Trisha would be the perfect addition to the household.

"The boys seem to like you," Jonathan said as they sat in the sitting room again, sharing another glass of wine.

"They're both great kids. You've done a wonderful job of raising them."

Jonathan laughed and shook his head. "You can thank Grace for that one!"

"Is Grace your wife?"

"Oh no! Grace was our previous nanny. She decided to retire down in Florida to be near her grandkids. Jackie was my wife. She was diagnosed with a terminal cancer when the boys were young…"

"Oh, I'm so sorry to hear that." Trisha's face flushed as she looked away.

"And I'm sorry I have to be so blunt about it. The boys still struggle with our loss, and as their nanny you'll need to be ready to support them. I probably should have told you this during the interview…"

He sighed and closed his eyes for a moment.

"I hope you can see why I'm in need of a good nanny. The boys are a handful, and I've poured myself into my work for so long that I can't do this alone."

Trisha nodded, her chocolate eyes locking on his once again. Her face was lighting up. Maybe it was the prospect of a challenge, or maybe she just felt bad for him. Either way, Jonathan could tell she wanted the job.

"Should we talk about your compensation?"

Her eyes widened as she stared at him. "R…really? You... you're not going to interview anyone else?"

"I had interviews all morning. Do you see any of them here tonight? You were the one who stood out. And after seeing how the boys took to you so quickly… I don't see a point in questioning fate… at least… if you're still interested in the position."

Jonathan clenched his fist as he waited for Trisha to respond. He wanted her to say yes. It was more than just his need for a nanny though. He'd enjoyed Trisha's company tonight, even if he spent most of the evening watching her talk to the boys.

"I'm definitely interested." She grinned broadly, her pearly white teeth showing. That made Jonathan grin in return.

The two of them finished off the bottle of wine as they ironed out all the boring details. Trish would start tomorrow, meeting Jonathan at the office after her classes ended. They'd pick the kids up from school together so he could walk her through their schedule. Friday morning, she'd be on her own.

If everything went well, she'd move in over the weekend.

Jonathan wasn't sure who was more excited, him, or her...

As she walked up to Mr. Ashcourt's office, Trisha wondered if her nerves would ever calm down. She'd already gotten passed two interview stages, yet as she went up to meet him before they picked up the kids from school, the butterflies in her stomach were doing backflips.

*God, I'm like a girl going on her first date*, Trish thought when she stepped off the elevator. When Mr. Ashcourt's secretary greeted her, she was taken back to her middle school days, feeling every bit of her youthful awkwardness and hoping he'd like her.

It stupid, really, since she'd already gotten this far. As long as she didn't do anything majorly wrong, like dumping more hot coffee into his lap, she had the job in the bank.

So why couldn't she shake her nerves?

When she stepped into the office and Mr. Ashcourt's bright green eyes locked onto her, she knew why. She couldn't help but develop a small crush on him. He was handsome, polite, successful, and available…

She hoped to God she'd get over that before she did something stupid.

There was no way Mr. Ashcourt would appreciate being hit on by his nanny. That sort of thing only happened in those drug store romance novels with muscular gods on the covers.

This definitely wasn't a romance novel, and she certainly wasn't no bombshell babe waiting to be swept off her feet. This was real life and fairy tale endings didn't happen. She had a better shot with Brandon and he was gayer than the front row of a Katy Perry concert.

"Good afternoon, Trisha!" Mr. Ashcourt smiled at me. "Why don't you have a seat on the couch? I'm just finishing up some last minute things, then we can run to get the boys from school."

"Sounds good." Trisha tried to smile and look like she

wasn't nervous as all hell. Since Mr. Ashcourt didn't comment, she assumed it worked.

She pulled a paperback out of her bag and tried to read while she waited, but her eyes kept drifting over to Mr. Ashcourt as he worked. The man was focused on the papers spread out on his desk, thankfully, so he didn't notice the extra attention.

She watched him taking notes on a small legal pad and wondered what had him so absorbed in his work. Hell, she didn't even know what he did. She knew he was the CEO of AshCorp, but what AshCorp did, she wasn't quite sure. She made a mental note to Google him later and see what came up.

Twenty minutes later they were heading down to the office garage, Trisha following Mr. Ashcourt like a lost puppy. Thankfully, she was able to hold back her gasp when she saw his gorgeous Porsche sitting in his designated spot. Damn, even when he had to pick up his kids from school, the man did it in style.

Like a true gentleman, he loaded her small suitcase into the trunk, then the two of them were on their way toward the school. Trisha tried to pay attention to the route, but was thankful for GPS. There's no way she'd be able to find it on her own!

"I forgot to tell you," Mr. Ashcourt said as he wound through streets that seemed much narrower than they should be. "There's a car at the house for you to drive. Consider it one of your employee benefits."

Trisha nodded, slightly relieved. Her old Ford Taurus would've stood out like a sore thumb in this private school carpool lane… but she still found herself in disbelief. Did he seriously just *give* her a car to drive? For a moment she wanted to ask what kind of car it was, but thought better of it. Best not to look a gift horse in the mouth.

They had to wait a couple minutes, but soon, Declan came running toward the car, Alexander was trailing not far behind him. Trisha stepped out of the car, pushing the front seat forward so the boys could slip into the back.

The moment Declan was in the car, he started talking a mile a minute about his day at school. Trisha tried to focus on what he was saying, but the kid could've been an auctioneer. When she looked over at Mr. Ashcourt, they locked eyes and he shrugged, showing he was just as lost as she was.

Finally, Alexander had enough and elbowed his

brother. "Will you be quiet for once? You haven't stopped talking since you sat down!"

Trisha snorted, glad it was someone other than her that spoke up. She made a mental note not to give the kid sugar, fearing he might vibrate into another dimension from all the energy.

Declan pouted and crossed his arms, but he didn't complain.

When she glanced at the boys in the mirror, she saw Alexander had put his arm around his brother and Declan was leaning against him. She smiled at the sight. It was good to know they could be honest with each other without holding a grudge.

Driving up to the house was once again filled with wonder. She'd seen places like this on TV and in magazines, but had never before been even close to an architectural wonder like this. It was leagues beyond the tiny two-bedroom house she grew up in.

Briefly, she wondered how long it would take before she was no longer mesmerized by the sight of the place.

Still in the role of the gentleman, Mr. Ashcourt helped carry her small bag inside, even though she'd told him it wasn't necessary. Though, she had to admit, it was nice having a man treat her like this…

Mr. Ashcourt gave her a tour of the house and introduced her to the other staff. Gretta was a portly older woman who handled all the cooking. She was friendly and welcoming, and Trisha knew they'd get along just fine.

Judith, on the other hand, didn't seem to like Trisha one bit. Oh, she was polite for sure, but she was cold and distant. Luckily, Trisha wouldn't have to deal with her much.

Once the tour and introductions were done, Mr. Ashcourt led Trisha to her accommodations. The 'suite' he was providing her was more of a *house* than a bedroom. It had its own private entry that lead outside, a gorgeous bathroom, a kitchenette with everything she'd need to whip up a simple meal on her own, and it even had a small living room. Before she had a chance to acquaint herself with the space, he opened up a door and ushered her through. She blinked when he turned on the lights, revealing the attached private garage.

He pulled a set of keys off the hook by the door and handed them to Trish. "It's all yours," he said, pointing at the black SUV.

Trisha stared open mouthed at the car. It was a brand new BMW X5, looking like it'd just rolled off the lot. This was the kind of car rich soccer moms drove, not broke college students. "Are… are you sure?" she asked, looking between Mr. Ashcourt and the car. She could only imagine how much it would cost if she scratched it or something.

He nodded. "Of course. I wouldn't expect you to use your car while you're working."

"Th..thank you!" she said, looking down at the ground. She'd expected a moderately used car, not something this expensive!

Mr. Ashcourt grinned and chuckled. "It's no problem! Grace, our old nanny, had a car provided for her too. In fact… I let her keep it when she retired."

"You let her… keep it?"

"Like I said, consider it one of your benefits. Work hard and do a fantastic job caring for my children, and you'll be richly rewarded for your effort. Besides… it's a tax write-off."

He laughed, but she was still in shock. Trisha slipped the key into her pocket quickly, as if she were worried he might take it away and tell her it was all a big joke.

They headed back inside, Trisha's head on a swivel as she continued to take everything. When they left the garage behind and made their way back into the dining room, both boys were seated at the table, books and papers sprawled out in front of them.

"Okay, boys. I've got some more work to do, so I'll be up in my study. Trisha is in charge for right now, so if you need any help with your homework or anything, ask her." He turned and winked at her. "Good luck!"

The boys smiled, then turned back to their homework. For a moment, Trisha just watched them, wondering if she'd had that much homework when she was their age. She decided that she didn't, since she couldn't remember it ever taking very long before she was curled up with a book after school.

Trish retrieved her own backpack, then took a seat at the table with the boys to lend them a hand.

The boys were quiet as they worked. The only time either of them spoke was when Declan would ask his brother a question he wasn't sure about. Surprisingly, Alexander was patient with his little brother, explaining everything like a professional.

*I never had near that much patience*, Trisha thought as she watched the boys work together. She could have easily interjected and given Declan a hand, but this seemed like a very good habit to reinforce.

Once they were finished their homework, they passed it over to Trisha to check. She was actually impressed how well they both did. She started taking notes on their work, coming up with a plan to improve their study habits.

She was still at the table when Mr. Ashcourt came downstairs. "The boys abandon you already?" he asked with a laugh.

"They finished their homework and ran off to play one of their games." Trish saved her notes on the laptop, then stretched. "I checked it over for them, too. They're both extremely smart, you know…"

Mr. Ashcourt beamed proudly, then pulled out a chair and sat across from Trisha. "That's always nice to hear. Don't get too excited though. Today was a good day; they must've been trying to impress you. Last week I almost drove myself crazy trying to keep them in their chairs long enough to finish their work. Especially Declan. You've seen how much of a ball of energy he is."

"I can imagine how much of a struggle it must've been," she smiled at him. "You're a brave man, Mr.

Ashcourt."

"If you're going to live in my house, you should probably start calling me Jonathan. Anyway, it wasn't too bad. I got to spend a few weeks enjoying some time with my kids. It's going to be hard to get back to business-as-usual."

"Sounds like I've got my work cut out for me."

"Oh you'll be fine!" Jonathan said, waving off my concerns. "The boys already like you, and that's the hardest part."

*Well, at least someone has faith in me,* Trisha thought to herself.

The two of them chatted easily for a while longer until Gretta came from the kitchen and told them dinner was nearly ready. Jonathan headed up to change out of his work clothes while Trish stowed her school stuff in her room and retrieved the boys from what looked like a cutthroat game of Overwatch.

"Dad," Alexander said, his mouth full of food. "Zack has a birthday party on Saturday. Can I go?"

Jonathan thought for a moment, then nodded. "I don't see why not." He glanced over at Trisha. "Would you mind taking him shopping after school tomorrow so he can pick up a gift?"

"Sure, no problem." Trisha smiled at the two of them.

"Then it's settled. I'll drop you off at the party on Saturday, and Declan and I can have some fun together." He winked at Declan who grinned back at him.

"What about Trisha?" Alexander asked.

"I'll be packing my stuff up so I can move in here." At least, that was the plan. Jonathan had already arranged with a moving company to bring everything here Sunday afternoon, this way she'd be all ready to go full time on Monday.

"Cool!" He grinned at Trisha, then went back to his dinner.

After everyone finished eating Gretta's delicious meal, the boys dragged Trisha to their game room, pleading with her for help getting past a level on a strange little game called Cuphead.

Trisha only meant to play for a little while with them, but before she knew it, it was their bed time. Jonathan walked her back to her room after they'd sent the boys to bed.

"The boys really do like you," he said as they headed up the stairs.

"I think they just really like playing video games," Trisha replied with a grin.

"It didn't look like they were holding you hostage in there!"

The two of them laughed. She figured if playing a few games helped her bond with the kids, who was she to say no?

When they reached Trisha's room, they stopped outside the door. She looked up into Jonathan's eyes, her heart pounding. Out of nowhere she had the overwhelming desire to lean in and kiss him. She buried that feeling as deep as she could and put on a smile instead. *Where the hell did that come from?* She thought to herself.

"It really is going to be great having you here."

Trisha wasn't sure what to say so she just kept smiling, her cheeks heating up. "I might not see you tomorrow before I go to work, so, good luck! Don't hesitate to call me if you need anything."

"Thank you," Trisha said, trying to calm her pounding heart. "Good luck at work."

Jonathan then turned and walked away, Trisha's eyes still locked onto him. Even in casual clothes, she could see a nice firm ass, and her mind was going into over-drive as she wondered what he looked like naked.

God, first day on the job and she was *already* flirting with the boss…

## ❧ 8 ❧

### JONATHAN

Sleep evaded him. By time he crawled out of bed around five that morning, he felt like he hadn't rested at all. No matter how hard he tried, he couldn't get her out of his mind.

*Trisha…*

Since it looked like sleep was no longer on the menu, he went downstairs and made himself a quick breakfast. Gretta was still in bed, so he was left fending for himself. Luckily he wasn't completely useless when it came to cooking. He'd never be a chef, but he wouldn't starve either.

After a quick meal and some coffee, he headed into work, getting out of the house before Trisha woke up. He told himself it was to get a jumpstart on all the work that'd been piling up, but he knew it was a lie. He was trying to avoid seeing the woman. There was something about her that kept her running through his mind. That mocha skin.... Those chocolate eyes... God, she was fucking gorgeous!

The entire drive to work, all he could think about was Trisha. What the hell was wrong with him? He'd never thought about *any* of his other employees like this before. And he'd had plenty of them throwing themselves at him, trying to work their way up the corporate ladder.

He needed to distance himself from Trisha as much as possible. She had a job to do, and none of her duties involved satisfying his deepest desires. For the rest of the day he dove head first into his work. Luckily, she didn't call him for any questions, so that definitely helped keep her out of his thoughts. He even stayed late in the office, not leaving until around eight when he was nearly exhausted.

None of that helped when he finally made it home and found Trisha in the dining room.

Her laptop was open and papers were spread around her. For a moment, he just leaned against the door frame and watched her work. She was focused on whatever was on the screen and didn't notice him at first.

"Busy day?" he asked after a minute.

Trisha jumped and knocked a few of the papers onto the ground, making Jonathan chuckle to himself. He walked over and helped her pick them up.

"Sorry, didn't mean to startle you."

She ran her fingers through her hair, then smiled at him. Even looking frazzled, she made his stomach do backflips. "It's all right. My fault really."

"Yeah, it looked like you were lost in your work. Must be interesting stuff…"

"Fascinating, to be honest. I've been studying early childhood development and the role of growth in child psychology."

"Sounds like you really enjoy your work. Planning on being a child shrink when you graduate?"

"Maybe. I'm not sure exactly what I want to do. I've thought about a few different paths. All I know is I want to help people. There are so many kids out there who can't afford the kind of help they need. Most psychologists sit around listening to rich-people-problems." Her face almost instantly cringed and she looked down at the ground. "Sorry, I mean, no offense to you."

Jonathan laughed and shook his head. "I'm not offended. I've had to do my fair share of listening to *rich* people complain." He walked over and patted her on the shoulder. "I won't distract you from your work. I'm gonna see if Gretta left me anything in the kitchen."

"She said there were leftovers in the oven for you!" Trisha called as he walked into the kitchen.

"Thanks!"

Just like Trisha said, there was plenty of Gretta's baked ziti in the oven, just waiting to be heated up. Jonathan managed to scrounge up some Italian bread and a salad while the ziti heated up. He considered just eating in the kitchen, but he figured that would be a little too obvious if he avoided Trisha like that.

He had to make her think nothing was going on, lest she go running for the hills and leaving him stuck hunting for another nanny. So he brought out his bread and salad, along with a glass of wine and set it on the table.

Trisha was still knee deep in her school work, but her papers were no longer scattered about like they had been before. She was just as absorbed as she had been when he'd arrived though. She must've really be serious about her schooling, he realized.

As he ate, Jonathan studied Trisha some more. He found that he liked the way her brow furrowed as she concentrated. More than once he wanted to walk over and massage her shoulders to help relieve some of the tension.

Thankfully, Alexander came down into the dining room and helped push away those thoughts. He froze when he saw his father, then smiled and walked over to give him a hug. "Oh, hey. I didn't know you were home."

"Just got home not long ago. I was starving." He grinned at his eldest son. "I take it you came down foraging for food yourself?"

His cheeks turned pink, but he nodded, still smiling. "Yeah. I wanted a snack."

"Go on," Jonathan said. "Just not too much, okay? I don't need either of you getting sick."

Alexander nodded, then walked back over to the doorway. He stuck his head out, then yelled "Hey Dec, Dad's home!"

Trisha and Jonathan both looked at the boy, eyebrows raised. Neither had to speak for Alexander to blush and look down at the floor. "Sorry!" he said, before scampering off into the kitchen.

Jonathan shook his head while Trisha rolled his eyes. "I hope you weren't expecting this to be a quiet job," he said with a laugh.

"Oh, I gave up on quiet when we picked the boys up from school yesterday." She laughed as well. "They're certainly *boisterous*, aren't they?"

"That's putting it politely!"

Before Jonathan could say anything else, Declan came flying into the room, skidding to a halt a foot away from the table. If he'd stopped a second later, he'd have tumbled right into it.

"No running in the house!" Jonathan and Trisha said at the same time, grinning at each other.

Declan pouted, but walked over to his father and hugged him. "Sorry."

"I think there's an echo in here," Jonathan said, winking at Trisha. "I'm starting to wonder if you two need any more sugar!"

"Awww come on!" Declan's turned his puppy dog eyes on, pleading with his father.

"Okay, but no more running in the house, got it? Especially not when you're wearing socks. I don't feel like taking a trip to the ER tonight."

Declan nodded eagerly, and Jonathan thought his head might fly right off his small body. Maybe he really shouldn't give the kid any more sugar…

Then Alexander came back into the room, carrying two sodas and a bag of chips. He passed one to Declan.

"Don't be up too late, okay?" He eyed Alexander. "I want you both in bed before nine thirty. And don't forget, you've got that party tomorrow. Did you get a gift for your friend?"

"Yep!" Alexander said nodding. "And Trisha helped me wrap it, too."

"All right. Give me a hug, then you two go play. I'm gonna call it a night soon." The boys hugged him, then scampered off back into their little cave. He was starting to wonder if maybe he should push them to get outside more. Things were different than when he was a kid.

"Thanks for helping him today," Jonathan said, his focus once again returning to Trisha. It seemed like he couldn't go very long without returning to her. He was definitely going to need to head to sleep soon, before he did something stupid in his sleep deprived state.

"It was no problem." She looked up at him over the lid of her laptop and smiled. "It is what I'm here for, right?"

"That's true. But I still appreciate it." Not only had it saved him from having to wander around the store while Alexander struggled to make up his mind but it had allowed him to make some progress to get caught up at work. Even if he was about to fall asleep in his pasta now.

"I hope you don't mind that I'm getting a little work done here…" Trisha said a bit apprehensively. "I've been keeping an eye on the kids, but you did say that I'm off work at eight, right?"

"I'm sorry I got home so late. I do appreciate you keeping them in line."

"Well, it was easy enough. I sent them up to take a shower and spend a little time reading. Declan started on Harry Potter tonight. If they needed me, I would have put all of this away until they were asleep… of course…" Trisha replied.

After a few more minutes of small talk, Jonathan left

her to the stack of psychology papers. He stopped in and said goodnight to the boys, receiving hugs from both of them, then headed up to his room for a quick shower of his own.

As the warm water cascaded down his body, Trisha appeared in his mind again. He tried to push her out of his mind, but she stuck with him even as he finished up and dried off.

She hadn't been here two full days and all he wanted to do was bend her sexy little ass over the dining room table.

Maybe it wasn't such a good idea to hire her....

## 9

### TRISHA

"So, what's he like?" Samantha asked, grinning at Trisha. She'd been sitting on the couch waiting the moment Trisha walked in the door. Leave it to Sam to want gossip without delay.

"He's nice." Trisha set her purse on the counter and started looking around, wondering where to begin packing. They'd lived here for over two years now; it was strange to even be thinking of packing her things up.

"Nice?" Samantha snorted. "The guy's a billionaire! There's gotta be more to him than 'nice.'"

Trisha rolled her eyes as she walked into the kitchen. She wouldn't need any of her kitchen things, but she wanted to pack them anyway. The job wouldn't last forever, so she didn't want to toss everything. Worst case, she'd get a storage unit and pack some of this stuff away.

"What else is there to say? He's my boss, not my boyfriend." *I wish he was my boyfriend*, Trisha thought, not daring to say it out loud. "I don't see much of him. He works late. He didn't get home until almost nine last night, then he ate and went right to bed."

Sam snorted, and it was clear she was looking for more dirt. They both knew each other well enough to know when the other was holding back. To her credit, she let it drop, at least for now…

The two of them started sorting through all the different things, figuring out what was Sam's and what was Trisha's. The amount of stuff they seemed to have accumulated over the past few years was amazing. Most of it was Sam's, but they still had to go over everything to make sure nothing was missed.

Brandon and Justin showed up around noon with a case of beer and pizza for everyone. Even though Trisha wouldn't be that far away and would still see everyone, her moving day turned into a mini goodbye party for her.

After lunch, the guys helped her pack her things up. By the time the sun began to set, almost everything Trisha owned was in a pile of boxes in the living room. It was pretty depressing, seeing her room nearly barren. Even the living room and kitchen looked less like the home she'd known for the past few years.

"You okay?" Sam asked, walking up and putting her arm around Trisha's shoulders as she looked into the living room.

Trisha nodded, taking a deep breath. It'd take a bit of getting used to living somewhere else, to living with *someone* else. Sam had been her best friend growing up, the one who'd always been there for her.

Turning, Trisha wrapped her arms around Sam. "I'm going to miss you."

"I'll miss you too. But it's not like we're never going to see each other again. You're not that far away."

"I know, but between school and taking care of the kids, I don't know when we'll be able to get together for awhile."

"We'll make time, don't worry." She hugged Trisha tight. "We'll just have to reschedule Taco Tuesday."

"To what, Taco Saturday?" Trish laughed and shook her head. It'd be silly, but silly was fine if it meant she still got to see her friends.

That night, as she laid staring up at the ceiling, she realized it was possible this would be the last time she ever stayed here. After tonight, she'd be living with Mr. Ashcourt…. With Jonathan… It would be strange living in that giant house. Just spending two nights there had been strange. Would she ever feel as comfortable as she did here with Sam?

The big house creaked and moaned at night. Her apartment made noises too, but those were *familiar*. The ones in Jonathan's mansion were new and different and unsettling. It would take a while for her to get used to it, especially without having a familiar face just down the hall.

Instead, she'd have Jonathan just down the hall.

Maybe it wasn't all bad…

Even now she could see that handsome face when she closed her eyes. It didn't matter that he was ten years older than her or that he was so far out of her league that he might as well be on Mars.

And yet, she couldn't get him out of her head. In fact, being unobtainable just seemed to make him *more* attractive.

Or maybe it was the way he looked at her. She'd caught

him staring in the dining room, and spent the rest of her time trying to look like she was enthralled in her work so she wouldn't have to meet his gaze.

At the same time, all of this just made Trisha more anxious. What if she made a wrong move and he tossed her out? Sam would be looking for a new roommate soon, so it wasn't like she could just move back in here. If worst came to worst, she might even have to move back home…

*Maybe I shouldn't have taken this job*, Trisha thought as she stared up at the ceiling.

There was still time to change her mind. She could call Jonathan first thing in the morning and tell him she wasn't sure she could juggle the job and her school work. He'd understand… right?

But then he'd be in a bind, trying to find another nanny for the boys.

She liked Alexander and Declan. They were sweet boys, even if they were a bundle of energy, and if they really were suffering after Jonathan's wife passed away… another sudden change might not go well.

And… she really *did* need the money.

With her living at the house, she'd have very few

expenses. She wouldn't have to pay for food or rent or utilities. Hell, she wouldn't even need to pay for gas. Jonathan had given her a credit card to handle all her nanny-related expenses, gas included.

This really was a dream job, even if it wasn't *her* dream job. It wasn't like she'd ever come across something like this ever again, so why not ride it out? Even if she only stayed for six months, she'd come out on top. Six months of her salary with minimal expenses would pay for a couple years of college.

As sleep began to overtake her, she decided to stick with the job, at least for now. She'd just have to find a way to keep her attraction under wraps. He was her employer, not some guy on Tinder.

THE MOVERS SHOWED UP FIRST THING THE NEXT morning. Trisha watched as they loaded up everything she owned into the back of a giant truck.

Sam and Trisha stood out of the way as they worked, Trisha having packed up the last of her bedsheets that morning. Her bed would be another thing she'd have to put into storage, she figured, since her room at Jonathan's already had one.

Once all the boxes were gone, the apartment was even more depressing. Even with the living room furniture and Sam's things still there, the place just wasn't the same.

Trisha pulled Sam into a hug again, trying to fight back her tears. God, why did this have to be so hard? She was staying in the same town, maybe thirty minutes away if traffic was bad. So why did it feel like she was losing her best friend?

"Come on, it's not gonna be that bad," Sam said, patting Trisha on the back.

"I know, really I do. I just…. I can't help it."

Trisha sniffled and buried her face in Sam's shoulder. *I won't cry. I won't cry!* She told herself, over and over. She was determined not to let herself break down into tears.

After their heartfelt goodbye, Trisha was in the SUV, heading toward the house to meet the movers. Tears still stung at the corners of her eyes, but she refused to give in. This was a good change, she told herself. There wasn't any point in crying.

She pulled into the driveway just as the delivery men were opening the back of the truck. Once she showed them where everything was to go, she stepped aside and let them get to work. She had them just set her bed to the side in her room, planning to go out and rent a storage unit later that day.

She was sitting in the dining room on her laptop when she her feet clamoring down the hall. Seconds later, Declan came into sight, skidding to a halt when he saw her, his socks sending him sliding on the wood flooring.

"You're back!" he said with a grin. "Cool!"

"Yep, I'm back." Trisha grinned at the energetic boy. "The movers are just bringing my things in now. Where's your dad and Alexander?"

He pointed with his thumb over his shoulder. "In the game room. We're all playing Mario Kart. They sent me to get snacks. You wanna join us?"

Declan talked a mile a minute, and it took all of Trisha's focus to follow his words. She could only imagine how Alexander or Declan's teachers were able to keep up with this kid all the time.

"Once the movers are done, I'll come join you, okay?"

Declan nodded and grinned, then disappeared into the kitchen. Even from her spot at the table, she could hear him rummaging through cabinets and the refrigerator.

Moments later, he appeared again, his arms laden with junk food and sodas for everyone. He grinned at Trish, then was on his way back to the game room.

"Don't run!" she yelled after him.

Not thirty seconds later she heard a crash, wincing at the sound. Quickly, she ran out of the room toward the sound, finding Declan face first in the hallway, his bounty scattered out. *That* was why she'd told him not to run, especially since he was wearing socks again.

*Maybe now he'll learn,* she thought as she walked over to him.

Nothing seemed to be broken, at first glance. And there was no blood, though now Declan was moving, tears already forming.

"You okay?" she asked, squatting down in front of him.

He nodded, but still fought to keep from crying. "Dad's gonna kill me."

When he turned to look at the exploded cans of soda that were covering the hallway the dam broke and tears came flooding out. Trisha pulled him into her arms, gently patting him on the back. Her heart ached as the boy buried his face in the crook of her neck, bawling his eyes out.

"It's okay, relax. Your Dad won't be mad." She patted his back between each word. "Come on, I'll help you clean everything up, okay? It'll be good as new in no time."

It took a minute or two for him to calm down. Once he did, the two of them cleaned up most of the snacks, setting aside the bags of chips and stuff that hadn't been destroyed in his tumble. Then they grabbed the trash and took it into the kitchen.

"Where does Judith keep her cleaning supplies?" Judith was off on the weekends, so it was up to them to clean it themselves. Which was fine with her; the less interaction she had with Judith, the better.

"Over here!" Declan lead her to a small closet off the kitchen where she found most of the supplies she'd need. She handed Declan a broom, then grabbed the mop and a bucket. After she filled the bucket with soapy water, they headed back to the hall.

Declan swept up the bit of chips that'd been sacrificed, then stood out of the way while Trisha mopped up the soda. She'd gotten the majority of it when Jonathan appeared at the end of the hall.

"Uh oh. What happened here?" he asked, frowning as he approached.

Out of the corner of her eye, she saw Declan stare down at the floor, tears forming at the corners of his eyes again. She reached over and ruffled his hair, smiling at him when he looked up at her.

"Someone learned what happens when you run on hardwood floors in socks. Nothing broken though, other than a few sodas."

Jonathan sighed and shook his head. "I warned you about running in the house, didn't I?" When Declan nodded and looked at the floor, Jonathan sighed again. "You're lucky you didn't get hurt. You could've really done some damage, buddy. No more running, okay?"

Declan nodded, his head moving a mile a minute. Poor kid was going to give himself a concussion if he wasn't careful.

Trisha wondered how long the lesson would last. She had a feeling, in a couple weeks, he'd have forgotten his little spill and been right back to running around. It was a good thing kids were durable and resilient.

A minute or two later and the floor was shining like new. She was smiling proudly at her work when one of the movers poked his head into the hall.

"Ms. Holcut?"

"Hmm?" She turned to face him. In all the excitement, she'd completely forgotten they were even there! "Is everything okay?"

"Oh yes," the man said with a nod. "Just wanted to let you know we're finished."

"Oh!" she squeaked out. She passed the mop to Declan, who held the mop in one hand and the broom in the other. Then she dug out her wallet and handed the man a few bills as a tip. "Thank you so much!"

The man thanked her, then left. It was official now. She lived here.

It seemed to hit her like a sack of bricks. She wasn't quite sure how to react, knowing that she was living in a house that last week she'd thought she'd never even seen the inside of. Yet here she was, the newest resident of Ashcourt Manor.

"Can you play video games with us now?" Declan asked, his boyish voice jolting her out of her daydream.

"Sure!" She turned and grinned with him. "Let's go put this stuff away and get some new sodas. Then we can play!"

"Woo!" Declan actually jumped for joy, which made her laugh.

Jonathan shook his head and picked up the surviving snacks. "I'll meet you in the game room. No running this time!"

"Yes, sir!"

Putting her arm around Declan, Trisha led him back to the kitchen. She cleaned out the mop and bucket while Declan grabbed more snacks and drinks. When she was finished, she found him grinning at her, his arms loaded up with more stuff.

She sighed and shook her head, which was already becoming a common occurrence. She took some of the stuff from his arms, to help avoid another catastrophe. Why they'd sent the smallest person to retrieve snacks, she'd never know. The again, what was the point of being a big brother if you couldn't use your little brother as errand boy once in a while?

Once they had everything, Declan lead the way to their gaming den. Alexander and Jonathan were in the midst of a heated race. Trisha watched as the two of them would bump shoulders, trying to knock the other off course. If she hadn't known better, she'd have thought they had money on the race from the way they were playing.

"Yes!" Alexander yelled, jumping up in celebration as

his character cross the finish line moments before Jonathan's. "In your face, old man!"

Jonathan dropped his controller on the couch and grabbed Alexander in a headlock. He then proceeded to noogie him as Alexander flailed and struggled to break loose of his father's grip. After a minute, Jonathan released the boy, grinning at him. "Who's the old man?"

Alexander stuck his tongue out, then flopped back onto the couch.

Declan had me sit on the other end of the couch, then grabbed a controller and handed it to me. Once he added the fourth player to the game, he sat between me and Alexander. It was a good thing he was tiny and Alexander was the size of a twig, since the couch was a tight fit for four people!

She'd played Mario Kart before. It was a staple of game nights with Sam, Brandon, and Justin. Still, playing with these guys was something completely different. Alexander and Declan were like pros at the game and even Jonathan kicked ass.

She came in last every single race. It was like she was cursed, unable to rank any higher than eighth. All three of them were cutthroat, knowing exactly when to use their items and where each and every shortcut was. A couple weeks of this and she'd be killing game night, that was for sure! Either that or she'd be too depressed to ever pick up the game again.

Before she knew it, the sun had started to set. Finally, Trisha set the controller down and shook her head. "Okay, I'm done! You guys are killing me."

Both boys protested while Jonathan just grinned. Then he looked at his watch and his eyes bulged. "Oh wow, it's that late already? I guess I should feed you two gremlins something other than chips and soda huh?"

They shrugged, having already started another race without Jonathan and Trisha. Jonathan just shook his head, apparently used to their gaming addiction by now. He looked over at Trisha over the boys' heads.

"Pizza okay with you?"

"Uh, sure." Trisha blinked at him, not sure what else to say.

Jonathan nodded, then stood and stretched. "Gretta gets the weekends off, so we're usually on our own. The only time she works weekends is if I'm going to be out of town, this way you won't have to worry about cooking. Normally I'll cook on the weekends, but tonight I just don't feel like it."

Trisha chuckled and smiled at him. That made a lot of sense. And, to be honest, she wasn't much in the mood for cooking either.

While Jonathan stepped out of the room to order pizzas, Trisha watched the boys race. She was pretty sure they had more road rage than any actual drivers.

A few minutes later, he stuck his head in the room. "Pizza should be here in 30. You mind watching these two while I shower really quick?"

"Sure, no problem!" That was her job, anyway. Although, she wasn't quite sure if she was she was technically on the clock or not. Either way, it wasn't of a hardship to sit and watch the boys play Mario Kart. In fact, it was actually kind of entertaining.

Jonathan wasn't gone very long. Well, more like she lost track of time again. When he came back, he wore a t-shirt and a pair of linen pants, a stark contrast to his normal outfit. On work days he'd been in a suit and tie or at least his dress shirt. Even this morning he'd had on a polo shirt and a pair of slacks.

It was a little jarring to seeing him dressed so.... casual.

He sat on the armrest and watched the boys play. Trisha had opted not to play any more with them, so she alternated between watching them play and watching Jonathan. The t-shirt was just a tad tight on him, showing just how fit he was beneath it.

It was all Trisha could do to keep from staring at him.

## 🜁 10 🜂

### JONATHAN

He'd put aside all of his work for the weekend, spending all of his time with the boys. While Alexander had been at his party and Trisha had been packing her things, he'd gotten a chance to spend time with just Declan, something that rarely happened.

Then he'd spent Sunday with both boys, playing video games for almost the entire day. He couldn't remember the last time he'd played games for that long. Normally if he played with the boys it was only for an hour or so.

By the time he'd gone up to shower, they'd completely exhausted him. But at least with his mind focused on the game, he was able to keep from ogling Trisha. Plus, it helped that they were on opposite sides of the couch, the boys sandwiched between them.

But after his shower, he didn't have that distraction any more.

He thought about how Trisha had handled Declan's accident. Nobody was able to get through to Declan when he had a meltdown… but Trisha *did*. She'd calmed him down, then helped him clean everything up.

And she'd done it all without getting angry with him.

He'd really lucked out finding her. Now he just needed to keep himself in check so he wouldn't send her running for the hills. He kept reminding himself that she was his employee, just like everyone at the office. Trying to make this anything more would be a huge mistake.

Now he just needed to get the *rest* of his body to understand that.

He was thankful when the doorbell rang. He nearly ran from the room to get the pizza from the delivery driver. But when he turned around after tipping the driver, Trisha was standing there in the hall. His heart skipped a beat, his mouth going dry.

"Can I help?" she asked, smiling at him.

It took all of his will power not to drop the pizzas to the ground and pull her into his arms. He pushed those thoughts away and tried to return her smile without raising any suspicion of his true thoughts. "Sure! Can you grab some plates and napkins from the kitchen? I figure we'll eat in the game room. Throw on a movie or something."

"Absolutely!" There was that grin again, then she headed toward the kitchen, leaving Jonathan staring after her like a lost puppy.

*Get it together*, he told himself.

Dinner was its usually affair, Declan talking a mile a minute, even with pizza stuffed in his mouth. It was a wonder the boy never choked on his food, since he didn't stop talking even when he was eating. He was like some tiny miracle. A tiny *very loud* miracle.

When Jonathan called it a night and headed back upstairs, he was both pleased and annoyed at choosing Trisha to be the new nanny. She really was great with the boys, and even Alexander had warmed up to her.

Yet, on the other hand, he was clearly falling for her. Maybe he should've gone with one of the women who'd been old enough to be his mother. Then, at least, he wouldn't be thinking about what Trisha might look like bent over the kitchen counter.

It was a good thing he had a lot of work to do with AshCorp. With the new hospital project, he'd be busy enough to occupy his mind. Maybe after a week or two, he wouldn't be so infatuated with this woman…

11

# TRISHA

As the weeks went on, Trisha developed a routine. She'd get up in the morning, have breakfast with the boys, then take them to school before going to her class. After class, she'd pick them up, they'd do homework together, and after the boys would disappear into their game room most nights.

Most nights, Jonathan got home around dinner time, ate, then disappeared into his study or his bedroom. That was fine with Trisha, since it seemed like every time she saw him, her heartrate quickened. The less she saw of him, the better, she figured, since it kept her from doing something stupid.

And with the boys not being all that young, she didn't have to watch them like a hawk. She was essentially a glorified insurance policy. Her job was to be there if either of the boys needed anything and to make sure they didn't burn the house down.

That, and driving them all across the city.

All in all, it was a pretty easy job. Every once in a while Declan would throw a fit over something, but between her and Alexander, it didn't take long to fix whatever was wrong. They were good kids.

As the semester approached its end, Trisha was apprehensive to say the least. She was glad to be finishing another year of school, but that also meant the boys would be out of school as well. What was essentially a part time job would turn into a full-time job and then some.

But, at least she hadn't signed on to take any courses over the summer. That would help.

The week leading up to her finals was the most stressful one of her career yet. Not only did she have her exams, but Jonathan had to fly out to California for a few days, leaving her alone with the boys for the first time.

It wouldn't be much different than normal, since he was only home in the evenings anyway. Still, it was

nerve wracking knowing she'd be completely responsible for both boys while their father was gone.

The boys were sad when he left, but when the three of
them drove home from the airport, the boys had gone
right back to talking about video games. Apparently
they'd gotten used to him going away ages ago.

Once they got home, they ran to their game room
while Trisha grabbed her laptop and set up at the
dining room table. It'd become her little office while
everyone else was busy, since it gave her easy access to
the kitchen and she'd be able to hear if the boys yelled
for her.

That was pretty much how they spent the entire week.
Trisha would work, the boys would play, and the house
survived being burnt to the ground. Having Judith
handling the cleaning and Gretta handling cooking was
a godsend though.

Judith didn't seem to enjoy having Trisha around.
Every time they were in the same room together, Judith
seemed to glare at the younger woman. Trisha couldn't
think of anything she'd done to personally offend the
woman, so she just shrugged it off.

Meanwhile, the boys kept her from overdoing things.

Before she knew it, her finals were over and Jonathan was back from his trip. All of her anxiety and nervousness were for nothing, since neither boy was any worse for wear, other than a scrape on Declan's knee from where he'd fallen running to the car after school.

The boy never seemed to learn his lesson. Trisha figured he just had way too much energy to be able to just walk somewhere. Judging by the way he was always bouncing up and down, it didn't seem to be too far from the truth.

Jonathan was pleased, at least she thought he was. But after the first night, which he spent with the boys while Trisha went out with her friends, he went right back to work, with Trisha barely seeing him at all.

She was starting to think he was avoiding her.

And honestly, that kind of worked for her. It kept her from flirting with him, even if it was just with her eyes. Every time he joined them for dinner, Trisha was unable to look away from him. It was a good thing he was always so tired after work, since it meant he didn't notice.

"Why don't you just say something?" Sam asked as they sipped margaritas at the bar. Brandon and Justin were on vacation, leaving just the two of them for their get together this time. "Ask him out. Maybe he feels the same way."

Trisha snorted. The guy was loaded and gorgeous. Like he'd ever be interested in his nanny of all people. Besides, he was like ten years older than her. What could she have that would possibly interest him, other than a pair of tits?

"Yeah, right. He'd probably toss me out before he finished laughing." Trisha took a sip of her margarita, then closed her eyes and sighed.

She'd expected her crush to fade as time went on. She figured it was like her fascination of Ashcourt Manor. Once she got used to it, the marvel would fade. Sure, the house was still impressive, but now it wasn't something that took her breath away to look at.

Jonathan, on the other hand…. He still made butterflies appear in her stomach every time she thought about him, never mind saw him. It was a miracle the guy hadn't picked up on her infatuation yet. Him working so much was definitely helping.

"You never know until you try."

"Do you hate your new roommate that much?" Trisha

asked, grinning at Sam. "Is this your way of asking me to come back?"

Sam had waited a few weeks, just in case Trisha's job hadn't panned out. Then another girl moved in, an acquaintance of Sam's that'd broken up with her boyfriend and needed a new place to live. Which meant if Trisha made a move on Jonathan and he sent her packing, she had nowhere to go except back to her parents.

She'd started building up a good bit of a nest egg, since she had so few expenses living at Ashcourt Manor, but she needed that to pay for her schooling, especially with grad school looming on the horizon. Besides, it wasn't like she could find a place to live instantly if she suddenly found herself on the outside looking in.

"Ashley's nice," Sam said after drinking some of her margarita. "You'd like her."

"Then bring her one day when we hang out. It's not like Taco Sundays are so exclusive you can't bring a friend."

"Maybe I will! She has been a bit of a shut in. I think she's still trying to get over that asshole Trey. I can't believe the fucker cheated on her. He should have his balls cut off."

Trisha snorted. That was Sam all right, never afraid to speak her mind or defend a friend. It was going to take one tough guy to sweep her off her feet. Trisha didn't envy any of the ones who'd tried in the past.

"I don't know why you're being so hard on yourself," Sam said a few minutes later. "The guy isn't going to blow a gasket just from you checking him out. Hell, he'd probably get a kick out of it. You know how much guys like to have their egos stroked."

That was the understatement of the year.

"I'm surprised he hasn't made a move on you already. Aren't guys like him *always* supposed to be screwing their secretaries and nannies? Isn't it, like, in the contact you sign when he hires you? You know, I read a book once where this rich guy has a sex contract…"

"I'm not going to *fifty shades* with this guy!" Trisha smacked Sam in the arm. "And maybe he's not interested in me."

"Oh please. What's not to be interested in? You're *gorgeous*. And smart, and funny, and sweet. Don't go selling yourself short."

Trisha looked down at her drink. Sam had said all that before, but she still had a hard time believing any of it.

Sam downed the rest of her margarita, then tossed a couple dollars into the tip jar before pulling Trisha away from the bar. "Come on, let's go for a walk. You could use some fresh air to help clear your mind."

Walking around did help, at least a little bit. The city was always so full of life, even on a Sunday evening. It definitely helped rejuvenate her a bit. This silly little crush on Jonathan wouldn't be the end of the world.

This wasn't her first unrequited love. She'd get over it, just like all the rest. Until then, she'd just keep her cool like she'd always done. It wasn't like she tried to jump into the pants of every guy she'd ever liked.

"Carla, can you start looking into flights for me? I'm going to have to go out to Italy for a little while to sort things out."

Jonathan stacked up the papers he'd been looking at and set them aside. He was going to have to go visit with some of his investors in person, if he wanted their money. And if he wanted his project to go forward, he would need their investment.

Besides, it was a trip to Italy, even if it was a business trip. It was hard to argue with perks like that, even if he did have to put up with an endless stream of paperwork!

Carla nodded and scribbled something onto her notepad. "Just for you?"

Jonathan opened his mouth to reply, then stopped. He didn't need any other employees out there, but why not take Trisha and the boys? It'd been a while since he'd had an actual vacation with the kids. If he extended his stay for a little while, he'd be able to spend some real, quality time with them.

Plus, he figured Trisha and the boys could enjoy some time in the sun while he was working. It'd be better than them sitting out home while he was away.

"Actually, hold off on that for a day or two. I might bring the kids with me. I think we're overdue for a little vacation time."

Carla snorted. "I've been telling you that for ages. Just let me know and I'll get the tickets. Anything else for today?"

"No, I think that's it," Jonathan said, shaking his head. "I'll let you know if I need anything."

Carla smiled and left, leaving Jonathan to his thoughts. Would Trisha even want to go on the trip? Heck, he didn't even know if she had a passport. And it wasn't like he could bring the boys without her. Not unless he wanted the boys wondering around a foreign country alone while he was at work.

He decided he'd broach the subject at dinner tonight. Well, if he made it on time, he thought as he glanced at the clock. He'd be late for dinner every night for the past week.

That meant he needed to stop daydreaming and get to work, if he planned on getting out of here on time.

That night, he walked in the door just as Gretta was putting food on the table. She glared at him as he took off his suit jacket and sat down. Jonathan smiled sheepishly at her, apologizing for being late.

Gretta grunted and finished serving the food, then winked at him before she disappeared. He'd told her numerous times to sit and enjoy the meal with them, but she never did. He knew she'd be in there packing up some food for herself and her husband, so they could sit and have dinner together, even if it would be a little late in the evening.

"How is everything?" Gretta asked when she returned with a bag.

"Delicious as always," he told her with a wink. "I don't think you've ever made anything that hasn't tasted heavenly."

Gretta waved off the compliment, despite everyone else chiming in to tell her how wonderful everything was.

"You just leave the dishes in the sink and I'll take care of them when I come in in the morning. And there's a pie in the fridge, if anyone is still hungry after."

Jonathan stood and hugged Gretta before she left. "You're wonderful, you know that?"

"You just remember that when it's time for my Christmas bonus!" she said, laughing as she left. That seemed to be a running joke with his emploees.

After she was gone, Jonathan decided to broach the subject with everyone. "So, in about two weeks, I'm going to have to fly out to Italy for a few days to meet with some investors."

Alexander and Declan both groaned. "Do you gotta?" Declan asked.

Jonathan nodded. "I do. But, I was thinking, maybe you guys would like to come along. I'll spend a few extra days after the meetings are over and we can have a little vacation."

That cheered both boys up. They both bounced with excitement, talking about different things they'd like to do. They'd gone with Jonathan to Italy about three years ago and sounded eager to go back. While they chatted together, Jonathan turned to Trisha.

"Will you be able to go? Do you have a passport?

Trisha blinked at him. "Me? Uhhh… Yeah, I have a passport. But why do you want me to go?"

"Someone has to watch the boys while I'm in meetings." He winked at her. "I figured you'd enjoy a trip to Italy as well. Have you ever been?"

Trisha shook her head. Then, she looked down at her plate. "No, but I don't think I can afford it."

"Oh, don't worry about that." Jonathan waved his hand. "I'll pay for it. You'll be taking care of the boys while we're there, so it's no big deal. I mean, if you'd like to go."

"Oh, I'd love to go!" she said almost immediately. "I just feel weird, having you spend that much money to fly me out to Italy, just to watch the boys during the day."

Jonathan smiled. It was kind of sweet, actually. Most people would've jumped at a chance for a free trip to Europe. This was the first time he'd ever had someone hesitant to go. But she really would be doing him a favor by keeping an eye on the boys while he was working. It was either that or have the boys fly out later in the week, when he was finished his meetings. This way, the boys would get a longer vacation, even if he wasn't there for all of it.

"Don't worry. The company will pay for it, so you don't have to feel weird. Besides, after everything you've done since you started, you deserve a bit of a vacation, too."

The boys must've overheard our conversation, since Declan chimed in. "Please, Trisha! You gotta go with us! It's gonna be so much fun!"

"Well, I can't really say no to that," Trisha said with a laugh. She grinned at Declan, then Jonathan. "It looks like I'll be going with you then.

"Perfect!" Jonathan clapped his hands together and returned her grin. "I'll have Carla book tickets in the morning then."

The rest of dinner was filled with excitement as everyone chatted about the upcoming trip. Jonathan filled Trisha in about where they'd be going and the things they could do while he was working. Alexander and Declan both chimed in at certain parts, telling stories of their last trip or just mentioning things they were excited about.

"Where will we be staying?" Trisha asked. "A hotel?"

Jonathan shook his head. If it was just him, he stayed at a hotel near work, since that was the most convenient. But he'd discovered long ago that if he had the boys with him, it was much easier to rent someplace larger.

"Our company owns a villa just outside of Naples. We'll stay there."

Jonathan grinned when he saw her eyes go wide. He knew visiting Italy would be an experience she'd never forget, and he was excited to bring her along. It'd been a while since he'd travelled with anyone other than a co-worker.

When the boys were younger, he'd taken them on his trips abroad frequently. But in the last few years, Grace hadn't been up to traveling, so they'd stayed home while he traveled. Now, he'd get to bring the boys on a real vacation again. Plus, he'd have Trisha to keep him company as well.

He couldn't wait.

## 13

### TRISHA

Trisha eyes had been wide and her head on a swivel since they stepped off the plane. She'd had a passport since she was a child, but this had been her first chance to use it. And this wasn't a quick jaunt to Canada or Mexico. She was on a completely new continent!

Plus, she hadn't been crammed in sardine can with a hundred other people. They'd flown on the AshCorp company jet, which meant they'd had the entire plane to themselves. The boys had even been able to watch a movie during the flight.

Jonathan had been on his laptop most of them, while Trisha had opted to read. She'd gotten behind on her reading since signing on to be a nanny, so the long flight was the perfect time to catch up. She'd have read a lot more if she hadn't stopped to gaze at Jonathan every few minutes.

Even experiencing her first trip on a private jet, she still couldn't get him out of her head. The man was like a drug, one she was inexplicably drawn to.

As they drove through Italy toward the villa, her face was almost glued to the window as she tried to take in all the sights. She couldn't wait to get out there and explore Italy! She'd always dreamed of visiting Europe, of seeing all the historical sights and tourist locations. Now she was finally getting a chance to live that dream, at least partially.

But no matter how fascinated she was, she couldn't stop glancing over at Jonathan every once in a while. He seemed to have a perpetual smile on his face ever since they'd gotten off the plane. At least she wasn't the only one excited, she thought to herself.

Not that she'd worried about that. Alexander and Declan had been bouncing off the walls since last night.

"What should we do first?" Declan asked as he leaned passed Trisha and looked out the car window.

Trisha shrugged. The boys had spent the last week

detailing all the things they could do in Italy, and she didn't have a clue where to start. There was so much to do. So much to see! Where were they supposed to begin?

Luckily, Jonathan came to her rescue. "How about we just relax at the villa tonight? You guys can walk down to the beach while we get acclimated to everything. Then we can go out to dinner."

That would work. The day was already half over, so it was a perfect way to wind things down. Besides, once they got to the villa, they could sit down and plan out what they wanted to do and when for the next week and a half.

She'd already decided she needed to visit Rome while she was here. It just wouldn't be right to visit Italy and not spend at least a day in Rome. According to Jonathan, the ancient city was close enough for a day trip.

Then again, compared to the US, everything in Europe was pretty close together.

When the driver pulled up outside their villa, Trisha's eyes widened for the millionth time that day. The place wasn't huge, nowhere near the size of Ashcourt Manor, but it was still a spacious little place. It sat right up against the beach, with the closest neighbor a good bit away.

It looked like something plucked straight out of a beautiful painting.

She made a mental note to get Sam an amazing gift while she was here. If it wasn't for Sam going behind her back and sending in an application for this job, she'd never have gotten to experience any of this. She'd be in Sam's debt for a lifetime!

The villa was definitely better than a hotel. Trisha and Jonathan both had their own rooms, while the boys shared the third. Each bedroom also had its own private bathroom. Plus, there was a spacious kitchen and dining area, and a living room with a large TV. But the cherry on top was the sliding glass doors that lead onto a porch with a perfect view of the beach.

Even from the doorway, Trisha could see the waves crashing against the shore. When Alexander and Declan ran down to the water, Trisha had to fight not to do the same thing. For a few moments, she felt like a kid again, in a magical world.

But she was here to be an adult. It was her job to keep an eye on the boys, not act like a kid herself.

Trisha and Jonathan both sat on the porch and watched them. They were close enough to keep an eye on the boys but far enough away that the boys wouldn't feel smothered by their watchful eyes.

"So, what do you think so far?" Jonathan asked.

"It's gorgeous!" Trisha couldn't fight the smile that spread across her face. "I can't wait to really explore everything tomorrow. I've always dreamed of visiting Italy one day."

"It really is a unique place. I wish I could stay here tomorrow and show you around. But the number for the driver is on the fridge, in case you need him. Please don't be afraid to call him, either. His whole job is to be a chauffeur and tour guide when executives come to visit. We may as well get our money's worth!"

"Thank you. I really appreciate you bringing me along for this."

"You don't have to thank me. In fact, I should be thanking you. If you weren't here, I wouldn't have been able to bring the boys along, and it's been a while since we've been able to go away together. Grace wasn't a big fan of flying."

The two of them talked, and before Trisha knew it, she

was getting lost in Jonathan's eyes. The sun was setting on the horizon, but she barely noticed it as she looked into those glistening emeralds, so different from her own brown eyes. Even the shouts and laughter from the boys started to fade away.

Then, Declan's ear piercing scream broke her daydream. Both her and Jonathan stood and turned to look out at the boys, watching as Declan popped up from the sand, coughing and sputtering while Alexander laughed.

When they realized neither one was hurt and it was just a bit of playful roughhousing, they sat back down with matching sighs of relief. Trisha chastised herself for getting so caught up in Jonathan. Like he said, she was here to watch the boys.

She'd been able to keep a lid on her feelings and this beautiful place wasn't going to be her undoing. She would keep herself under control, no matter what.

Thankfully, Jonathan would only be with them in the evenings. That would go a long way to helping her push those feelings aside. At least until the end of the week when he was finished with his work.

That would be the real challenge.

## 14

### JONATHAN

The sun came up way too early the next morning. He still hadn't adjusted to his new time zone, even though he'd gone to sleep early the night before. Jonathan wished he could sleep in a little, like Trisha and the boys could.

He'd also much rather have been heading to visit Rome today, rather than meeting with some stuffy old men. But he needed those stuffy old men, so he didn't have much of a choice. Besides, the whole reason they were in Italy was because of these meetings.

So after a few minutes of grumbling, he slipped out of bed and into the shower. A hot shower helped wake him up a little, but he was still going to need a good bit of coffee if he wanted to function properly. After his shower, he made himself a large cup for the road just as his driver pulled up.

Despite relying on the caffeine to keep him functioning, the meetings had gone well. So far, his potential investors seemed intrigued with what he had planned. After a quick conference call with some of the guys back in Atlanta, he headed back to the villa.

Trisha and the boys were still out, so he grabbed a beer and headed to the back porch to watch the sun set. Even if he did have to work, there were much worse sights to come back to after a long day in the office.

Watching the sun set over the Italian coast was much different than seeing it set in Atlanta.

He must've drifted off because the next thing he knew, the sun had completely set. The front door shut and he jumped, rubbing the sleep from his eyes. Trisha and the boys trailed into the house, laughing at something.

He stood and stretched, then went in to greet them. "Have a fun day?" he asked as he yawned.

The boys nodded and Declan launched into an epic regaling of all the sights they'd seen today. The boy seemed even more energetic than normal. Alexander even chimed in a few times to add to Declan's story.

Trisha just smiled and let them talk, though it was obvious she'd enjoyed herself just as much as they had. Jonathan was glad he'd brought them all along. They deserved a bit of a vacation. Especially Trisha, having to take care of the boys all the time. Even if she still had to watch the boys while they were in Italy, he was sure a change of scenery was appreciated.

When the boys were finally tired out, Trisha offered to get them tucked into bed. That gave Jonathan a minute of peace to reflect on the day. He was staring out the glass doors at the ocean when she walked up beside him.

They stood there in silence for a few moments, just enjoying the marvelous view. Then, before Jonathan could stop himself, he asked "Would you like to go for a walk?"

## 15

### TRISHA

The picturesque moonlight beach took Trisha's breath away. It was like nothing she'd ever seen. She hadn't gone on many vacations growing up, so this was like something out of a fairy tale. The beach had been gorgeous during the day, but now it was simply amazing. Sand glittered in the moonlight. It almost looked like the stars had fallen to Earth.

"Are you enjoying yourself?" Jonathan asked, startling her out of her day-dream.

"Yes! The kids have me running all across creation to see things, but I've had so much fun." Trisha sighed and looked out at the ocean again. Her first trip to Italy was something she'd never forget, that was for sure, and it'd barely begun. "I'm sorry you haven't been able to join us."

She'd hoped to spend some time with him on the trip, but she knew she couldn't really complain. This was a business trip.

Now that she thought about it, this was the first time they'd really been alone together in months. Sure, they'd passed each other in the halls back home or been in the kitchen at the same time, but never for more than a few moments. The only time she really spent time with him was during meals, when the boys were present. If neither of them were home, he always opted to eat in his study while he worked. She was starting to think everything he did was business-related.

He didn't ignore the boys though. On the weekends he was in town, he spent them with the family. Those were usually Trisha's days off when she'd go visit with Sam or Brandon or Justin, so she never really got to see Jonathan in 'dad' mode. Maybe that would change on this trip.

As she looked at Jonathan silhouetted in the moonlight, she was glad to be here.

And maybe a little nervous. After all, this was the closest she'd had to a date in months! Sam kept trying to set her up with one of their friends, but she couldn't get Jonathan out of her mind. Every time he walked into a room or she passed him in the hall, her heart would beat a bit faster and her hands would get a bit clammy. It was like a schoolgirl crush… and a little sand between her toes wasn't helping anything!

"I'm sorry I haven't had much free time, but I'm almost finished with my work here. With any luck, I'll be home with you and the boys in a couple days, and we'll have a few days to enjoy." He grinned at her, and her heart began to hammer.

God, would she ever get over this stupid crush? It was a miracle she hadn't screwed things up yet. If she wasn't careful, he'd realize her gaze was just a bit too friendly and he'd give her the boot.

And yet, as they walked in relative silence, Trisha found herself drifting closer and closer to him. She was like a moth being driven toward his flame. No matter how hard she tried, she couldn't pull away.

When they stopped to look out at the gentle waves crashing against the sand, she stood only a few inches away from him. She could feel his body heat, even on this warm night. She wanted to press against him and feel his arm around her shoulders.

He turned to face her and when she looked up into his eyes, her breath caught in her throat. He'd always been gorgeous, but standing here now, he was heavenly. Slowly, she moved toward him, her eyes closing and lips parting just slightly.

Time slowed to a crawl until her lips pressed against his. Fireworks exploded inside her and she pressed her entire body against his. When he wrapped his arms around her and held her tight, she thought she might melt into him.

She had no idea how long they stood there, kissing like teenagers, but when a particularly strong wave crashed against the shore, the cool water hitting their bare feet, they jumped apart.

Trisha stared at him, her eyes wide. She hadn't just done that. No way. She hadn't just kissed her boss. "Oh god!" she said at last, her voice having risen an octave. "I'm so sorry! I shouldn't have done that!"

When she turned to run back to the villa, he grabbed her wrist and pulled her back against him. His arms were around her waist again, holding her tight against his strong body. He looked into her eyes, his emerald gaze once again mesmerizing her.

"Don't be sorry." His voice was like velvet, making her

shiver as it washed over her. "There's just something about you, Trisha… I can't help myself, no matter how hard I've tried."

He brushed a strand of hair out of her face, then leaned in and kissed her again. The world began to spin as they kissed, Trisha's legs wobbling beneath her. If Jonathan hadn't had his arms around her, she'd have crumpled into the soft sand.

Again, they were both panting when they broke the kiss. This time though, Jonathan didn't let go of her. As they stood there, staring into each other's eyes like lovers, she could feel something pressing against her body. For the second time, her breath caught in her throat as she realized what it was.

*God, he must be huge*! Trisha thought to herself. She should've pulled away, should've run back to the villa and locked herself in her room until morning. Even if he was gorgeous and clearly turned on, she shouldn't have been doing this. He was still her boss!

But she couldn't bring herself to move. She stood there, letting him hold her, her heart threatening to pound right through her chest. With how tight they were pressed together, she knew he could feel every single beat.

"I *need* you, Trisha," he said, his voice gravely now. "I've needed this for so long."

She knew exactly what he meant. She'd needed this as well. How many lonely nights had she spent in bed, thinking about him? How many times had he invaded her dreams, doing all sorts of sordid things to her?

Now she wanted him to do those sordid things in real life too.

"I want this too," she said, her mouth dry. Her face flushed, and she knew, even in the darkness, he'd be able to tell.

"We… we should go back to the villa," he said before giving her another quick kiss.

She leaned her head against his chest. She'd have gladly let him have his way with her right out in the open if that'd been what he wanted, but when he took her by the hand and led her back down the beach, she followed along eagerly.

Her mind raced with all of the possibilities. She had no idea what Jonathan had planned for her, but she didn't care. She just wanted to be with him, to be touched by him, to be held by him. Whatever he wanted, she would gladly give him.

Even with their quickened pace, the walk back to the villa seemed to take longer than it had coming out. The universe was screwing with her, making her wait as long as possible before she'd get what she craved.

Quietly, the crept into the villa, locking the sliding glass door. The last thing either of them wanted was for this to be interrupted. Jonathan lead her to his room and she kicked the door shut.

The door hadn't even closed before she was in his arms again, their lips pressed together in urgency. They both wanted this. No, they both needed this. Neither of them could deny their feelings any longer now.

"God Trisha," Jonathan said, sounding breathless. "You're the most gorgeous woman I've ever seen."

She ran a finger down his chest, feeling the contours of his muscles beneath the thin t-shirt.

Jonathan took her hand and held it in both of his until she looked back up into his eyes. "I've never been with a woman like you before. Smart, gentle, kind, delicious..." He leaned in and kissed her again.

Now her heart really did try to burst free from her chest. "Please… Jonathan… I need this…"

"Your wish is my command." He gently kissed her

hand, then let go and pulled his t-shirt off, making her gasp at the sight of his toned body. He really *was* a god come to life!

But before she could say anything, his hands were on her, pulling off light sundress over her head, leaving her in nothing but her bra and panties. Immediately, she felt self-conscious, but when he pulled her back into his arms and kissed her again, she lost all inhibitions.

He didn't even break the kiss as he unhooked her bra and let it fall to the ground. Nor did he break it when Trisha reached between them and began to undo his pants, letting them drop to the floor as well. When he kicked them off and pulled her tight against him, she could feel his hardness pressing against her, only his silk boxers separating them now.

God, he felt even *bigger* than before.

"Are you sure about this?" Jonathan asked after breaking the kiss.

All Trisha could do was nod. She couldn't speak any more, her mouth and throat having gone dry. Even her brain was full of fuzz and static.

Gently, Jonathan pushed her toward the bed. When the mattress hit the back of her knees, she sat down,

Jonathan now towering over her. But he didn't stay there long. Instead, he dropped to his knees in front of her.

When he slipped his fingers into the waistband of her panties, she lifted her hips and let him pull them down. Her face was hotter than ever as he spread her legs and got his first look at her nakedness. It'd been so long since a man had seen her like this, she'd almost forgotten what a thrill it was.

He didn't waste any time before leaning in and kissing along her hidden folds, making her moan out in pleasure. She had to clamp a hand over her mouth to keep from waking the boys as Jonathan continued to kiss and lick her.

Soon, his fingers were working their way inside her, gently at first, then with more intensity. It was all she could do to keep from moaning too loudly. Jonathan was incredibly skilled, bringing her closer and closer to the point of no return with every single calculated touch.

Legs on his shoulders, she laid back on the bed, squeezing her eyes shut. She'd imagined this many times over the past few months, but none of her dreams even came close to the real thing. Her dream man was nothing compared to this god in front of her.

"Oh fuck," she breathed out through gritted teeth. "God, I'm almost there."

Her breath came in gasps now, her hands balled into fists around the bedsheets. Fire began to pool into her veins, coursing through her body all at once. She fought to hold on as long as possible, but it wasn't much use. Jonathan was far too good for that.

Then, in a blinding flash, her entire body seemed to explode. "Oh god!" she yelled out, much louder than she wanted two. Her hips arched up off the bed and she grabbed Jonathan's short hair, pushing him tight against her. She shook and spasmed as her orgasm rocked through her body.

For a moment, she thought it might last forever. Then it was gone, and she was laying in the bed again, trying desperately to catch her breath. Stars floated before her eyes as she gazed up at the ceiling. Even from just that, she was worn already, her body completely exhausted.

But when she let go of Jonathan and he stood up grinning at her, his lips glistening with her juices, she found her second wind. She shuddered at the sight of him, his black silk boxers tented obscenely.

God, she couldn't believe how turned on he was making her right then. He'd just given her an explosive orgasm she'd never forget, and already she wanted more. *Needed* more. She needed more than just his fingers and mouth. She needed him inside her.

"Fuck me," she breathed out between pants. "Please, Jonathan, I need it."

He leaned over and kissed her, his hardness pressing against her again. "I've been waiting to hear those words," he said, that rich voice washing over her once more. She'd never get tired of hearing him talk, especially that close to her, with barely anything between them.

When he stood up again, he pushed down his boxers and revealed himself to her for the first time. Her heart seemed to stop in her chest as she took in every inch of him, from his chiseled torso, to his long, thick manhood, down his sculpted legs.

Fucking hell.

He was way more man than she'd ever had, in more ways than one!

But, as she stared at him, there was no place she'd rather have been. And when he stepped forward and leaned over to kiss her again, the fireworks returned, echoing through her entire body. She wrapped her arms around him and held tight, feeling his bare hardness sliding against her.

God, she couldn't wait to feel him inside her! If he was even half as good as he'd been with his tongue and fingers, she knew she was in for the ride of her life.

After a few moments of making out, their tongues eagerly exploring the other's mouth, Jonathan broke the kiss and grinned at her. He reached down and stroked himself, Trisha watching as her breath hitched in her throat.

"Fuck me," she said, her own voice hoarse and desperate.

She didn't have to ask him again. He lifted her legs and pulled her until she was right at the edge of the bed. Moments later, she felt him right at her entrance, gasping as she slowly pushed his way inside.

As he slid into her, inch by inch, her entire body seemed to be on fire. He fit perfectly, stretching her to the absolute limit like their bodies had been made for each other. By the time he'd pushed his entire length in, she felt complete for the first time in her life. They were like two puzzle pieces, locking together into one.

It wasn't until Jonathan leaned down and pressed their lips together again that he really began to fuck her. She gasped and moaned into his mouth, her hands wrapping around his neck and head.

There's no way she'd have been able to contain her moans. She'd had only a tenuous control over herself earlier, but now, that control had gone completely out the window. His kisses were the only thing muffling the sounds of their passion.

Each time he thrust into her, jolts of electricity shot through Trisha's body. That familiar fire began to envelop her again, bringing her closer and closer to the finish line with each passing second.

Jonathan moaned into her mouth. His hips moved faster and faster, his fingers digging into Trisha's soft flesh. Neither of them would be able to last much longer.

Trisha tried to hold on as long as possible, but she just couldn't do it anymore. Tendrils of fire lashed out against her insides as the world around her began to spin. Every muscle in her body contracted at once, her pussy clamping down on Jonathan's massive cock like a vice.

He thrust into her one last time and she could feel the

tension reach its peak. Even with her mind soaring a million miles away, she could feel his cock throb and pulse inside her as he came.

For a few blissful moments, Trisha thought she'd died and gone to heaven. Then, she came crashing down to Earth, gasping for air, her heart pounding. When Jonathan broke the kiss and smiled down at her, she thought she might melt right into the bedsheets.

"You're amazing," he said, his voice low and deep.

Trisha shook her head, already feeling the flush rising in her cheeks. "No, you were amazing."

Jonathan kissed her again, this time just a gentle peck on the lips. When he pulled out of her, Trisha gasped and whimpered. Emptiness filled her now, and she crossed her arms over her chest as a cool breeze wafted over her.

She turned and saw the door to Jonathan's balcony had been left open. She hoped no one had seen or heard them together. They'd done their best to be quiet, but there was only so much you could do.

Jonathan didn't seem worried in the least. He simply crawled into the bed and pulled Trisha into his arms.

As she lay her head on his chest, he lifted the now ruffled blanket and slid it over the two of them.

With Jonathan's arms wrapped tightly around her, it was like all of her problems and worries just disappeared. And as she closed her eyes, she no longer cared about anything except this moment.

❦

Sunlight washing over her woke Trisha the next morning. She could hear birds chirping in the distance as she rubbed the sleep from her eyes. Her brain still foggy, she couldn't figure out where she was for a few moments.

Then last night came crashing into her all at once. She turned to look at Jonathan, only to realize he wasn't there. His side of the bed had long since gone cold, meaning he'd been up for awhile.

Trisha frowned and pulled the blanket tighter around her. Why hadn't he woken her before he'd left?

She leaned back against the headboard and sighed. She wanted to believe he'd left quietly because he hadn't want to disturb her. But what if he realized they'd made a mistake?

Trisha was just the nanny. She wasn't a trophy wife or a celebrity, and she certainly wasn't some wealthy debutant. She'd grown up just outside the projects in a house that lived paycheck to paycheck. She was nothing like any of the other women Jonathan had dated.

Even now, she could see the photos of him with girls on his arms from when she'd looked him up. They'd all been cut from the same cloth. Tall, slender, dressed in clothes that cost more than she'd make in a year… and they were *white*.

Was she just being paranoid? Maybe Jonathan didn't care about that sort of thing…

When she glanced over at the clock, she sighed again. She needed to get up and back to her room before the boys woke up. The last thing she needed was for either of them to figure out what had happened last night. If they saw her coming out of Jonathan's room wearing the clothes she'd worn last night, they might wonder what was going on.

She snuck back to her own room. Thankfully neither boy was awake just yet.

A hot shower helped wash away the memories of last night, but it didn't wash away the guilt. She'd let her lust get the better of her and slept with her boss. If he had second thoughts about what happened, this whole job might go up in flames. And besides that… she'd never used her body to get ahead in the workplace. What if he saw things differently? What if he thought she was trying to get more money out of him?

She'd really started to enjoy this job. The boys had grown on her and were kinda like younger brothers now. She didn't want to have to leave them.

But what choice would she have?

She'd just have to enjoy what was left of the vacation. It'd probably be the last one she'd take for a long time…

## ❧ 16 ❧

## JONATHAN

H e'd panicked that morning and he knew it. When he'd woken up with Trisha in his arms, he'd practically bolted out the door. He'd spent an hour sitting in a café, waiting until he could head to his meetings for the day.

Months had gone by with him keeping his distance from her and, in one night, he'd blown it all.

God, why couldn't he just keep his dick in his pants?

Going on that walk had been his first mistake. But it's been such a beautiful night and he'd needed to just unwind. He'd brought Trisha and the boys along to make this trip in the hopes of having a bit of a vacation, not to turn the nanny into a brand new sexual conquest.

So much for that idea.

He could avoid Trisha for today and even tomorrow, but after that, he'd need to face her. He'd planned to stay here for a few days after the meetings for a real family vacation, and yet, he was already thinking of excuses to go home early. He'd never felt like such a screw up in his life.

No, he'd have to stay here, at least for the boys. It'd be tough seeing Trisha and thinking about every single excruciatingly sexy moment they'd shared. How would he be able to look into those deep brown eyes without wanting to rip her clothes off one more time?

Trisha was gorgeous, even more so when he'd taken her to bed… and holding her in his arms had given him the best sleep he'd gotten in months.

All he could think about was Trisha. He faked his way through the meetings, nodding and agreeing to whatever was discussed. He may have been in the office but he sure as hell wasn't present.

The day dragged on and on. More often than not, he found himself staring at the clock and watching the hands tick around. Each second seemed to take a minute, each minute taking an hour. He'd even started to wonder if the day would ever end.

By the time he headed back to the villa that night, he felt like the entire week might've gone by.

He thought the villa was empty when he walked in. For a brief moment, he thought Trisha might've packed the boys up and gone home. Then he heard shouts and laughter drifting up from the beach.

He set down his briefcase, then crossed the living room to stand out on the porch. His breath caught in his throat as he stared out. Alexander and Duncan were out there, running around and playing in the surf.

But that wasn't what caught his attention.

Trisha was out there with them in a *sexy* little bikini. From the back deck he could see her dark skin glistening with water. Seeing her out there, running around and splashing with the boys…. All Jonathan could do was stand there and stare.

He wanted to just go out there and wrap his arms around her, but he was stuck and rooted in place. Out of the corner of his eye, he could see Declan jump onto Alexander's back and pull him down into an oncoming wave, both of them coming up sputtering after.

His gaze was locked immediately back onto Trisha, watching as she laughed and shook her head at the boys. As the boys splashed each other again, she turned and looked back at the villa, locking eyes with Jonathan. Neither moved for a moment, until Trisha shouted something to the boys and turned to walk up the beach toward Jonathan.

His heart pounded faster with each step she took. He wanted to turn and flee, but he was helpless. Besides, it'd be a little obvious if he ran away now. He just had to suck it up and deal with whatever came his way.

"How was work?" she asked as she walked up the steps.

Jonathan shrugged, tearing his eyes away from her to look out at the ocean. "Worse than you could ever imagine. I can't wait to be finished with these meetings."

"The boys can't either. You know, it's still early. Why don't you change and go spend some time with them before dinner? I'm sure they'd love to see you."

"That sounds like a good idea." He grinned at Trisha. Playing with the boys would be a great way to get his mind off the smoking hot nanny.

So that's exactly what he did. He went inside and changed into a pair of swim shorts, then headed back out. Trisha was sitting on the balcony, sipping a glass of wine while he went out to play with the boys. At least now he wouldn't be staring at her the entire time.

As he splashed around with the boys, everything seemed to fade away. It'd been too long since he'd done something like this with them. They'd done little things together at home, like going to a movie or mini-golf or something, but this was different.

It was a good bonding experience.

That's when he knew everything would be all right. No matter what happened with work, no matter what happened with Trisha, as long as he had his boys, everything would work out in the end.

When the sun began to set, the three of them headed back up to the villa. With Alexander at his side and Declan riding piggy back, he walked inside to find Trisha in the kitchen cooking dinner. She still had her bikini top but she'd pulled on a pair of shorts as well.

"You didn't have to do that." Jonathan said as he set Declan down. "You're not here to be our cook."

Trisha shrugged and smiled. "It's no big deal. I was in the mood to cook tonight!"

"Do we have time to wash off before dinner?"

Trisha nodded. "Don't take long though! Dinner will be ready in about half an hour."

Jonathan opted for a cold shower to help get himself under control. He was definitely going to need it if Trisha was going to keep wearing that bikini during dinner.

Not that he'd try to stop her. This was her vacation too. She deserved a chance to relax, and he wasn't going to complain about the view…

When he came out of the bedroom feeling refreshed, Trisha was just putting the food on the table. "Anything I can help with?" he asked.

"Can you get silverware out?"

"Sure!"

Dinner was ready and the table was set and the boys still hadn't reappeared. Jonathan frowned at their bedroom door, wondering what was taking them so long. Trisha stood to check on them, but Jonathan shook his head.

"You sit and relax. I'll go get them."

Trisha look surprised, but took a seat at the table nonetheless as he made his way upstairs. Jonathan could hear the boys talking and laughing inside their bedroom. He knocked on the door and the room went silent.

"Yeah?" Alexander finally shouted.

"Finish up in there. Dinner's ready."

"Okay!" he shouted again.

Jonathan rolled his eyes. Letting those two hide behind a closed door almost always led to shenanigans. He wondered what they were talking about.

"Everything okay?" Trisha asked when he walked out of the bedroom.

"Yup!" He smiled at her. "Just the boys being boys. They'll be down in a minute."

Trisha laughed and nodded. "They're both good kids though. And good brothers. Alexander has been a huge help with Declan."

"He hasn't been giving you too much trouble, has he?" Declan could be a real handful when he wanted to.

"Oh no! He's just a good old fashioned eight-year-old, you know?"

The two of them laughed. Jonathan knew exactly what

she meant. He loved both of his sons dearly, but there were moments when he just wanted to stick his head in the sand and disappear.

A few minutes later, the boys finally emerged from their room, their short hair still wet. They grinned and laughed at some inside joke neither of the adults probably would've understood even if they'd asked.

"About time you two showed up," Jonathan said, eying the two of them.

"Sorry. Declan hogged all the hot water," Alexander said, gently shoving his brother.

Declan stuck his tongue out and pushed Alexander back.

"Okay, okay," Jonathan said, holding his hands up. "Let's just eat. Trisha prepared a wonderful meal for us, so no arguing at dinner."

"Sorry," both boys chorused at once.

The rest of dinner went by without incident. Trisha had prepared a delicious lasagna that was to die for. She must've gone shopping while Jonathan had been at work, since she even had fresh bread and a salad to go along with dinner.

"That really was amazing," he told her as they cleaned up. "I didn't know you could cook like that."

Trisha shrugged, her face flushing. "It was nothing, really. Gretta could out cook me any day."

"Gretta could out cook anyone!" Jonathan said with a laugh. "But this is still the best damn lasagna I've ever had."

Once the dishes were done, Jonathan went over and sat on the couch next to the boys. "Going to watch a movie with us?" he asked, looking over at Trisha.

"Oh, I don't think so. I'm getting pretty tired."

"Aww come on! Please watch with us!" Declan said, pouting at Trisha. "Pleaseee!"

"Well, how can I say no to that?"

Jonathan chuckled. There wasn't much use arguing with Declan once he set his mind on something. The kid was like a terrier, not willing to give up without a hell of a fight. Trisha probably saved herself a good bit of headache by just agreeing.

Declan moved over on the couch, forcing Alexander even closer to Jonathan. Then Declan looked up at Trisha and grinned at her until she sat down next to him. He passed Alexander the remote and let the two boys decide what to watch.

After a minute of arguing, which earned both of them a stern look from Trisha and Jonathan, they finally settled on a superhero movie. Apparently Trish wasn't the only who was tired, because two thirds of the way through the movie Alexander was leaning against his father, barely keeping his eyes open.

When Jonathan looked over at Declan, he saw the smaller boy leaning against Trisha, her arm around him as he slept. He smiled at the sight, his heart swelling as he watched the two of them.

For the first time in years, he felt like he had a *complete* family, and that scared him. He liked Trisha, but was he ready for this kind of commitment? No one would ever be able to replace Alexander and Declan's mother, but if he started to get serious with Trisha, would they feel like he was trying to?

When the movie ended, Jonathan sent Alexander to bed, the boy wobbling on his feet as he walked. Then, carefully, he carried Declan into the bedroom and laid him down.

Trisha was cleaning up a few things the boys had left out when he returned. For a moment, he just stood there and watched her. "I think we should go for another walk…" he said, the words leaving his mouth before he could process them.

She looked up at him, a surprised look on her face. Then she frowned.

"I mean, you don't have to, if you're too tired." He wanted to give her an out so she wouldn't have to come up with some other excuse to turn him down.

"N..no. I… I'd love to." She said at last, a shaking smile forming.

The two of them walked along the beach in silence, the crashing waves the only sound for what seemed like miles. There were other villas along this strip of beach, but they were spread out and the few they passed were quiet. It was like they were on their own private beach.

Trish was the first one to break the silence. "I'm sorry about last night," she said, her voice low.

He turned and blinked at her. What was she sorry for? She hadn't done anything wrong. Far from in, it fact. She'd done everything right last night.

"For what?"

"For… for coming on to you. For not being able to

control myself. I'll understand if you want to find another nanny when we get back to Atlanta, but I want you to know… I didn't do this for the job. I just wanted… *you*… a little more than I should."

Jonathan stopped walking, grabbed Trisha's arm, and pulled her to stand right in front of him. He waited until Trisha looked up at him, their eyes locking in the moonlight. If he wasn't careful, he could easily see himself getting lost in those eyes.

"You don't have anything to be sorry about. You didn't do anything wrong…"

"You're my boss! I shouldn't have slept with you." She broke free from Jonathan's grasp and turned around, facing away from him. Her shoulders shook slightly, and Jonathan knew she was fighting back tears.

He stepped forward and wrapped his arms around her waist, pulling her tight again him. "Please don't cry. I mean what I said. You didn't do anything wrong, Trisha. Everything that happened last night. I never should've pushed you like that."

"You didn't push me!"

"Then why are you crying?" He hated seeing her like

this. It was as if he was being stabbed straight in the chest.

"I… I'm not," she said stubbornly. "I just… I love this job. I love taking care of those boys. I don't want to leave them."

"You don't have to leave them. They boys love you, too. A blind man could see that. We can forget last night ever happened. It never has to happen again."

He wouldn't push her into this if it wasn't something she wanted. She was a really great woman, one he enjoyed having around. He wanted to her to stay, even if it was just as their nanny and nothing more.

"But I want it to happen again!" She pulled Jonathan's arms off her and walked a few feet away, staring out at the ocean.

Now Jonathan was really confused. If she wanted everything that happened last night, why was she crying? Why was she so upset?

"Sometimes… when I was growing up… my mother had to do *things* to keep food on the table. I saw the kind of men she brought home. She did what she had to do."

"I don't understand…"

145

"I promised myself I've never let that happen to me. I'd never use my *body* to get ahead in life."

"Jonathan walked over to her and put his hands on her shoulders, gently kneading the muscles. He could feel the tension in her body "I would never ask that of you. What we did… we both *wanted* it to happen."

In response, Trisha turned and stared into Jonathan's eyes. Then, she stood on her toes and pressed her lips to his. It took all of Jonathan's will power not to untie her bikini top and strip her nude right there on the beach. All of her hesitation seemed to have vanished as she tried to touch every inch of Jonathan's body.

After a few moments, he broke the kiss. "Follow me."

Trisha nodded and let him lead her back up the beach. The two of them practically ran back. Jonathan's heart pounded and not from the exercise. Just the thought of Trisha in his bed again had his cock rock hard.

He couldn't wait to fuck her again.

The moment his bedroom door shut, he pulled her into his arms again. This time, he didn't hesitate to untie her bikini top and let it drop to the floor. Within seconds the rest of their clothes were on the floor as well. Trisha shivered in his arms as his hard cock pressed against her. He broke their kiss and moved to kiss along her neck, loving the feeling of her quaking where she stood. He couldn't wait to feel her shake as she came beneath him.

Already she was breathless and they'd barely begun.

"Are you ready?" he asked. When she nodded, he led her to the bed and carefully laid her down with her beautiful legs spread wide. Once he'd decided he'd teased her enough, he started kissing his way up her body, taking his sweet time.

The sound of Trisha gasping and moaning was music to his ears. Having her squirm and beg was just the icing on the top.

He was too horny for much foreplay, but a little bit would make it so much better when he finally let her come. She needed to be right at the edge, begging to come, before he'd finally give in. Having a horny woman begging to be fucked was just what he wanted.

Especially when she was as gorgeous as Trisha.

Jonathan loved everything about her body. From her curvy him to her full breasts to her mocha skin. There wasn't a single thing he'd change about her. She was the perfect woman in every single way.

"God, Jonathan..." Her voice came between gasps. Her chest rose and fell quicker and quicker each time he pressed his lips to her bare skin. "Please.... God..."

Gently, Jonathan bit down on one of her nipples. "Not just yet," he growled, then went back to kissing around her chest. Once he reached the other breast, he nibbled on her nipple just enough to make her moan.

It didn't take long before Trisha was whimpering beneath him. More than once she tried to put a hand between her legs, but Jonathan always pushed it away. He wasn't going to have her ruin his fun by fingering herself.

Oh no, he was going to make her beg to be fucked, beg for that release.

By the time he reached her lips again, Trisha had her hands balled into the bedsheets. When they started to kiss again, she wrapped her arms around him and pulled tight, not letting go of him for anything.

Their tongues dueled together as they kissed harder than ever. Jonathan's cock was throbbing now, just waiting for its own sweet release. He wouldn't be able to hold out much longer, but right now, he was thoroughly enjoying Trisha's need to touch him.

He knew exactly what she wanted but he wasn't ready to give it to her. Not just yet.

Pushing his hips forward, Jonathan rubbed his cock against her slit. Trisha gasped and moaned into his mouth as they continued kissing. When he reached between them and rubbed her clit, Trisha gasped again.

The longer he teased her, the closer to the edge she got. God, he loved making her moan and squirm like this. When he finally gave in to her pleading and slipped two fingers into her, Trisha thrashed against the bed. Then she wrapped her arms around Jonathan, her nails digging into him.

As his fingers slid in and out of her, her fingers clawed his back. He knew there would be marks in the morning, but he didn't care. He just wanted to feel Trisha come again, wanted to give her pleasure that no one else could.

Seconds turned to minutes as time stretched on. Jonathan kept his lips firmly against Trisha's, doing his best to muffle her moans. He didn't need her waking of the boys and ruining their night when they'd barely gotten started.

Then, she was there. Her hips thrust off the bed, her

IMANI KING

body shaking even more than before. Her arms tightened around him, pulling him against her chest. If he hadn't kept kissing her, she'd have moaned loud enough for their neighbors to hear.

He kept fingering her, faster now, stoking that burning fire inside her. Feeling her come beneath him nearly made him lose control, but he managed to keep a lid on things. There was no way he was going to let himself come that easily.

Oh no. He still had many plans for the rest of the night!

As Trisha came down from her high, Jonathan slowed his fingers, but didn't stop completely. Her aftershocks of pleasure were too enjoyable to completely stop teasing her. But, after a few moments, she gently pushed him away as she slumped back onto the bed, trying to catch her breath.

Jonathan leaned in and kissed her on the check, then smiled down at her.

"Amazing," Trisha said between gasps for air. "Are you gonna fuck me now or what?"

"Tsk tsk. In such a hurry, are you?" He kissed her

150

again. "We're going to have to work on your patience a little…"

Trisha shuddered at his words, but her lips curved into a smile. There was no denying how much she was enjoying being tormented by Jonathan. Even now, her skin was covered in goosebumps. He had to fight the urge to kiss his way back down her body again.

Instead, he kissed along her jaw line, making her whimper again. It didn't take long before she was squirming and begging.

"Please… Jonathan…. I *need* this!"

Those words were like magic to his ears. He kissed her on the check again. "Are you sure you're ready for round two?" When she nodded, he grinned.

This was going to be a fun night.

Jonathan brought his stiff cock back to her entrance, making her squirm as he rubbed the head up and down, teasing her once more. Sure, he wanted to just bury himself inside her, but there would be plenty of time for that. Right now, he was enjoying how she squirmed beneath him, whimpering as she begged to be fucked.

He brought his mouth to her breasts, suckling on one,

then the other, making her moan louder now. It didn't matter that she'd just come. She was on the edge again, and he knew it wouldn't take long to get her off for the second time that night.

Finally, Jonathan couldn't last any more. He needed to fuck her before his balls exploded. As much as he loved teasing her, even he could only take so much before he needed relief.

Grinning down at Trisha, he lined himself up with her, then leaned in and pressed his lips to her as he pushed himself inside. She moaned into his mouth, the sound thankfully muffled. Once his entire length was in her, he pulled his hips back, then forward again, not wasting any time building into a rhythm.

Trisha clawed at his back. For someone who had said no marks, she didn't seem to have any qualms about her fingers digging into him. Not that he complained. So long as Trisha was in his arms, she could do whatever she wanted to him!

That familiar fire in his stomach began to lash out at his insides. He grunted and closed his eyes, trying to fight it back, not yet ready for things to be over. It took every ounce of his will power to keep from coming right then and there.

He had to break the kiss, already out breath. He gasped for air as he looked down at Trisha, her eyes filled with lust. Just seeing her looking up at him with a fire burning inside her made Jonathan thrust faster now.

There was no way he would last much longer, no matter how hard he tried. But, on the bright side, judging by the way Trisha was moaning out, her body flushed, Trisha wouldn't' be lasting very long either.

Jonathan brought one hand between them and used it to rub her clit, bracing himself on his other hand. If he was going to come soon, he was going to make damn sure she did too. And thankfully, he knew each and every button to press to make Trisha come now!

It didn't take long before he had to bring his lips back to hers, just to muffle her moans. She was quickly approaching her orgasm, losing all control of herself. As they kissed again, her still moaning out, the fire inside Jonathan came closer and closer to exploding.

Somehow, he managed to hang on until Trisha came. She thrashed around beneath him. If he hadn't kept his lips pressed firmly against her, she'd have woken everyone in a five-mile radius as she moaned out.

Her pussy clamped down on his cock as he continued to thrust in and out of her. It became too much for him to bare, and finally, when he couldn't fight it any longer, he let go. He thrust into her one last time as pleasure tore through his body.

Every muscle seemed to contract at once. His toes curled, his hands balling into fists. His entire body shook as his vision began to blur. Stars swam before his eyes. The bedroom disappeared. Nothing but him and Trisha existed for those brief moments.

Then, it was gone, and he was left in a daze, gasping for breath. When he opened his eyes, Trisha was gazing up at him, a dopey grin on her face. Jonathan couldn't help but grin back at her. He leaned down and kissed her again, this time just a quick peck on the lips.

"Is there time for a round three?" Trisha asked with a giggle, her eyes dancing.

This woman was going to be the death of him!

But hey, who was he to say no to that invitation?

## 17

### TRISHA

When first rays of sun woke her the next morning, the first thing she noticed was Jonathan's arm still around her. She smiled up at the ceiling and snuggled closer to him, pulling the blankets tighter around them.

This was much better than waking up alone in a cold bed!

She tried to fall back asleep, but it eluded her this time. Even though she'd only gotten a few hours of sleep, thanks to their late night escapades last night, she was wide awake.

God... she'd never had sex like that before in her entire life. It was like Jonathan knew more about her body than she did. He knew all the right places to touch and kiss and lick. She'd never wanted to scream out that badly before.

It was a good thing Jonathan had been able to keep his head though. He'd done his best to muffle her moans and shouts with his lips, keeping them from waking the boys.

She couldn't wait until they were back in Atlanta. Then she wouldn't have to worry about the boys being right across the small living room from them. Back at the manor, she could scream as loud as she pleased.

She shivered as she recalled last night. She'd never known sex could be *that* earth shaking before. Sure, it'd always been good, but she'd never wanted to just melt into the mattress as her body threatened to turn into a pool of fire.

All the regret she'd had after her first night with Jonathan had disappeared. After their little chat last night, she no longer felt guilty about sleeping with her boss. These nights weren't about a boss and his nanny.

It was about a man and woman who both desperately needed the other.

She wanted to wake up every single morning in

Jonathan's arms. She wanted to fall asleep next to him, to have the comfort of his warmth to lull her to sleep.

Trisha's eyes shot open.

Fucking hell. She'd fallen in love with her boss.

This wasn't lust any more. This wasn't her seeing a hot man and wanting to ride him off into the sunset. If it was, she'd have been more than satisfied after last night. But she wasn't. She wanted more. *Needed* more.

And not just sex either, though she certainly wouldn't turn that away.

No, she wanted *him*. She wanted to be with him, for the rest of her life.

What the hell was she going to do now? What would Jonathan say if he found out this wasn't just a vacation hookup for her? Did he want the same thing? Or would she just go back to being his nanny when they returned to Atlanta?

And what about the boys? What would they tell them?

She closed her eyes again and groaned. Why couldn't things just be simple for once? Why did everything have to be so complicated?

Still wallowing inside her head, she didn't notice

Jonathan had woken up until he kissed her on the cheek and muttered "Good morning," into her ear.

She shuddered as his silky voice washed over her. Was it any wonder she'd fallen for the man? He was damn near perfect! Which just made it worse. He'd have the pick of any woman he wanted. He had no reason to want anything more from Trisha than a good night in bed once in a while.

Pushing those thoughts from her mind, she forced a smile onto her face. "Good morning. Ready for your last day of work?"

Jonathan nodded, a smile forming instantly. "More than ready. I can't wait to spend more time with you and the boys. There's so much I want to do." Jonathan's hand trailed up her body, telling Trisha exactly what he wanted to do.

"Don't you have to get dressed for work?" she asked, smirking at him.

He rolled over and glanced at the clock next to the bed, then turned back to her and pulled her tight against him. Trisha's heart thundered in her chest as he looked into her eyes, then slowly lowered his lips to hers. They kissed for both a moment and eternity, and when they pulled apart,

Trisha no longer had to force a smile onto her face.

"I still have time for a shower. Care to join me?"

Trisha's entire body flushed at the offer. But she found herself nodding anyway. Despite the turmoil inside her head, she wanted nothing more than to feel Jonathan's arms around her as hot water rained down onto their naked bodies. She'd have been a fool to say no.

When Jonathan threw the bedcovers off them and stood, pulling her gently to her feet, she giggled. Once they were in Jonathan's bathroom, he closed the door and pulled her into his arms again. He didn't kiss her though, just stared into her eyes and made her melt.

His hands on her ass and his arms around her waist, she didn't want to be anywhere else right that moment. No mattered what happened after this weekend, even if she never got to be with him again, she'd remember this moment.

She'd remember being happy and content and just a bit giddy.

"You still have to go to work," Trisha reminded him, smirking as she fought to keep from losing herself in his emerald gaze.

"I can call in sick." He smirked at Trisha. She smacked him on the ass, making his grin widened. "Oh… I like that. Going to punish me, are you?"

Now his eyes twinkled, making Trisha shake her head. This man was incorrigible! Although, she had to admit, a bit of role reversal would be kinda fun. But they didn't have enough time for that. Not only did he need to get to work, but the boys wouldn't be asleep much longer.

"Maybe tonight, if you're good." Trisha smirked at him, then winked before breaking the embrace.

She walked over to the shower stall, shaking her ass as she moved, then turned the water on. Immediately, water rained from the ceiling. His bathroom was much more impressive than her own, with a waterfall shower and a Jacuzzi tub. She'd definitely be enjoying these perks tonight, once the boys were in bed again.

When Jonathan wrapped his arms around her waist again, she could feel his hard cock pressed against her. Apparently he planned to enjoy a few perks this morning too! Well, if that was the kind of shower he wanted, she wasn't going to complain.

His hands went right between her legs, a finger slowly sliding up and down her slit. She shivered in his arms, a moan already slipping from her lips. She hoped he wasn't planning on having a lot of foreplay this time! Not only were they short on time, but she wasn't in the mood for being teased.

She wanted his cock in her right away.

Trisha turned and ran her hands up and down his glistening body. She licked her lips at the sight. Damn, he was one gorgeous man, especially when dripping wet!

After a moment of caressing his muscles, she stood on her toes and kissed him. Her eyes locked onto his and she grinned. "Fuck me," she said, her voice dripping with lust. She licked her lips seductively, being careful not to break eye contact.

That was all the invitation Jonathan needed!

His hips on her waist, he pulled their bodies together again. Then, he leaned down and kissed her with more passion than ever. Trisha's entire body was on fire as their tongues dueled for dominance.

When Jonathan broke the kiss, both of them were gasping for air. His cock was still rock hard, pressed against her soft body. God, if she wasn't so horny, she'd have been happy to be naked in his arms forever. But that could wait until after he'd given her the fucking she craved.

The fire in Trisha's eyes was reflected in Jonathan's as well. She wasn't the only one who needed this. When he placed his hands under her ass and lifted her off the ground, Trisha gasped. She tightened her grip around him, hoping he wasn't about to drop her onto the hard shower floor.

The next thing she knew, his hard cock was pressed against her entrance. Moaning, she laid her head against his chest. "Fuck me!" she breathed out, unable to keep from squirming in Jonathan's arms.

Jonathan kissed her on the cheek. "Aren't you impatient?" His breath was hot against her skin, even compared to the steam filling the room.

"Please…" she begged, wiggling her hips to rub her dripping cunt against Jonathan's cock. He sucked in a breath and Trisha grinned, knowing her little scheme was working. She continued to whimper and rub herself against him. "Please fuck me…."

Jonathan grunted and adjusted his grip. For a few moments, his cock was no longer in contact with her, which made her pout. Then, he lowered her slowly and his manhood began to slide into her.

Trisha closed her eyes and bit her lip to keep from moaning out. No matter how many times he fucked her, she never got used to having his long, thick cock inside her. He filled her like no other man had before. In a way, it was like his cock was made for her.

By the time he had his entire length in her, her body tingled. God, she wasn't going to last long, she thought. When Jonathan began to nibble at her neck, Trisha couldn't fight back her moaned any longer.

"You ready?" he asked, his lips only centimeters from her ear. All she could do was bite her lip and nod.

Jonathan's fingers dug into her hips as he lifted her slightly until just the head of his cock was inside her. Then he lowered in on quick motion, pushing his hips forward at the same time. Over and over he repeated the motion, using Trisha's body weight to fuck her on his cock.

Trisha's entire body was on fire now. The water cascading over them did nothing to quell it either. It took all of her strength to keep from screaming out as pleasure coursed through her veins. She hoped to God the kids were still asleep, lest they hear the sounds of their fucking.

Because as Jonathan built up a rhythm, it became

harder to keep quiet. She buried her face in the crook of Jonathan's neck to muffle the moans she couldn't fight back. Only one thing would satisfy her now.

She started to move in time with Jonathan's thrusts. Her nails dug into his back as Jonathan turned to brace her against the cool, tile wall. Now he moved faster, using the wall to keep her steady.

"Oh god!" Trisha moaned. The fire in her stomach began to bubble over as Jonathan fucked her. She wouldn't last much longer now… "Harder!"

Jonathan grunted and fucked her harder than he ever had. There was nothing romantic or loving about it this time. It was pure lust, two people who both just needed to get off. Raw, primal passion filled the air.

Seconds turned into minutes as time slowly ticked by. As the pressure inside her built up, threatening to explode, Trisha thought she might go crazy. She *needed* to come, but she sat teetering on the edge, unable to fall into the waiting abyss.

Both of them gasped for air as they approached the finish line. Trisha briefly wondered who would finish first, but she didn't have to wait long for an answer. Jonathan slammed into her, his cock throbbing, as he unloaded his seed with a guttural yell.

Feeling his cum splattering against her insides, Trisha lost control. Her entire body began to shake as her pussy clamped down onto Jonathan's cock, milking out the last of his cum. Stars swam in front of her eyes. Her fingers dug into Jonathan's muscular back.

For a few blissful moments, they'd both become a single being, united in their euphoric pleasure. Nothing existed except for one another. All sensations and feelings had vanished, replaced only by what seemed like never-ending happiness.

Then, it was gone, and they crashed back down to Earth, both gasping for air as the struggled to breath. If there hadn't been a constant stream of water cascading down their bodies, they'd have been stuck together with sweat.

Thank God for small favors, Trisha thought as she dopily grinned at Jonathan. Her head was still in the clouds. She wanted to stay in Jonathan's arms for the rest of her life. Finally though, he had to set her down.

*Well, at least he didn't drop me.*

Jonathan grinned at her, and she smiled back. "Well, was that what you were looking for?"

"Everything and more." Trisha stood on her toes and

kissed him on the lips. "Now, why don't you grab that bar of soap and wash me," she added with a wink.

Half an hour later, they were both drying off, grinning like fools. That had to have been the longest shower Trisha had ever taken. And yet, they'd spent very little time actually washing. It was more than worth the time though.

When they went back into Jonathan's room, Trisha froze. "Shit. My clothes are in the other room."

She wasn't much looking forward to putting her dirty bikini back on. At least, not now that she'd just gotten out of the shower. Nor was she keen on having another shower, unless Jonathan was going to be in there with her again.

Jonathan chuckled, his eyes going up and down her bare body. Judging by the grin on his face, that didn't seem like such a big problem to him.

"Don't even think about it," she said, eyeing him. "The boys are here, remember?"

Jonathan frowned but nodded. "I'd almost forgotten. It's still early. I doubt either of them are awake. Just wrap yourself in a towel and run back to your room."

He flashed her a grin. "Once I'm dressed, I'll come say good bye."

Well, that was a better plan than standing naked in his bedroom all day. Although, she could think of worse ways to spend her day than being spread eagle in his bed.

Once her towel was wrapped tightly around her body, she opened the door just a crack and peered out into the living room. The boys' door was still closed and she heard no sounds, so she quickly ran out to her own room.

Trisha could feel a flush creeping across her entire body as she prayed the boys were still sound asleep. The last thing she needed was for one of them to come out into the living room and find her wearing nothing but a towel!

But, moments later, she was safely in her bedroom with the door shut. That was two mornings she'd had to slink out of Jonathan's bedroom, which made her frown as she dressed. Part of her felt like a cheap hookup, creeping out before anyone knew she was there. But, deep down, she knew it was for the best.

The boys wouldn't be happy if they found out Jonathan

and her were sleeping together. She'd spent the last few months earning their trust and bonding with them. She didn't want all that work to go down the drain for nothing.

She really did care about Alexander and Declan, and she didn't want to hurt them.

The psychology student in her told her that dating their father would definitely hurt them. They'd see her as a replacement for their mother. But, in their eyes, no one would ever be able to replace her. Hell, she doubted anyone would be able to replace her in Jonathan's eyes.

## ✿ 18 ✿

## JONATHAN

For the rest of the week, Jonathan practically floated on air. His meetings went well, though they barely even registered on his radar. All he could do was count down the minutes in the day until he was back at the villa with Trisha.

This trip had been important last week, but now, it seemed like it was trivial. Then again, everything that wasn't Trisha seemed trivial. All the sights of Italy couldn't compare to her. Even when they were out on the beach, he could barely take his eyes off her.

He spent the evening with the boys, then as soon as they were in bed, he was in bed with Trisha. A part of his felt guilty about screwing her right across the house from the boys, but he shrugged it off. He was a man with needs, needs that hadn't been fulfilled in a while now.

And Trisha knew just how to fulfil those needs!

Besides, what would a little Italian hookup hurt anyone? It was just a bit of fun between two consenting adults. And it wasn't like he planned on ever letting the boys know anything about this week.

That was how the rest of the trip went.

He spent the days and evenings with Trisha, enjoying all the perks of a vacation in Italy. The boys were practically glued to his side all day, excited about actually getting to spend a vacation with their father. Even though his attention was constantly being drawn back to Trisha, he made sure he spent plenty of time with the boys.

He made a mental note to go on trips with them more often. Even if it was just trips around Georgia, he needed to spend a bit more time with them. They were only kids for so long. He didn't want them to grow up and feel like they were cheated out of a childhood with their father. It was bad enough they didn't have a mother any more.

Work took up a lot of his time, especially with the

hospital in full swing now. Money bought a lot of luxu-
ries in life for him and the boys, but it didn't buy time.
Which was why he was glad he'd decided to bring the
two of them on this trip.

But, each night after they went to bed, they were the
furthest thing from his mind. He had to admit, out of
all the sights he saw around Italy, Trisha was definitely
his favorite. And he enjoyed that sight in as many
different ways as he could – bent over the bed, up
against the wall, even out on his balcony. If he wasn't
worried about the boys waking up, he'd have fucked
her all over the villa.

By the time they boarded the plane for home, his balls
were running on empty. He'd never felt so exhausted
yet so content before in his life. That was one of the
benefits of a woman a bit younger than he was. Boy
could they fuck!

Unfortunately, their trip was over, which meant he was
back to being Trisha's boss, not her lover. It also meant
he was back to running a company. While Trisha and
the boys slept, he was on his laptop, once again diving
head first into work.

Now that he'd secured more investors, he could move
forward with his projects. The hospital was on sched-

ule, so he shifted focus to the surrounding area. He'd gotten quotes on the land, now he just had to start making offers.

He thanked God for whoever decided to put WiFi access in planes.

By the time they were back on the ground in Atlanta, he'd made a good bit of progress, though his eyes were beginning to droop. Unfortunately, the boys were wide awake now and as energetic as ever.

"When can we go back?" Declan asked on the drive home.

Jonathan chuckled and shook his head. They hadn't even gotten to the house and the kid already wanted another vacation. God, he wished he had that kind of energy again. "Maybe next summer."

"Awww!" Declan pouted. He crossed his arms in front of his chest and did his best to look as sullen as possible.

Jonathan just rolled his eyes. It wasn't like he could just drop everything and go on another trip across the world, just because Declan wanted to. Maybe he'd take the boys somewhere else before school started though.

Perhaps just a trip down to Florida. Disney World maybe.

Despite it being the middle of the day when he got home, he excused himself to get some sleep. Unlike the boys, who'd slept on the plane and didn't have anything to do tomorrow, he still had to get up and head into the office.

The joys of being an adult.

It felt strange to fall asleep without Trisha in his arms. In fact, it felt a bit lonely. But he pushed those thoughts out of his mind and forced himself to sleep. His fling with Trisha was fun, but it needed to come to an end.

He wasn't looking for a girlfriend or anything like that. He'd sworn he'd never marry again, at least not until the boys were grown. The last thing he wanted to do was bring another woman into their lives. He'd never be able to find a replacement their mother, and he wasn't going to try.

Not now, at least.

## 🏵 19 🏵

## TRISHA

"Y ou slept with him?" Sam's voice rose and octave, her words echoing around the apartment.

"Shush!" Trisha said, glaring at her. "Do you want the whole world to hear you?"

No one else was there, but she still didn't want Sam shouting about her sex life. You never know who might be walking past the apartment at any time. She wasn't ashamed of what had happened, but it still wasn't something she wanted spread around town. She liked her privacy.

Sam blushed and frowned, though her eyes still screamed for more information. "What happened? How? When? I need details, damn it!"

Shaking her head, Trisha filled Sam in on everything that had happened while they were in Italy. She spared some of the more intimate details of everything that had happened. She did have some modesty, even with her best friend.

Besides, she wouldn't want to make Sam jealous, now would she? Trisha smirked at the thought.

"But ever since we got home, he's gone right back to the way he was." Trisha sighed and leaned back against the couch, closing her eyes, the smile fading away. "I'd started to think just maybe this was more than a hookup to him. That maybe it meant something. I mean, I fell asleep in his arms almost every single night."

Even now, she could remember how it felt to have his strong arms wrapped around her. She remembered how content she'd felt every single night when she'd fallen asleep next to him. She'd never wanted those nights to end, though she should've known they would.

"Have you talked to him about it?"

Trisha shook her head. Every time she'd thought about talking to him during the trip, she'd gotten lost in his eyes and lost the willpower to broach the subject. She hadn't wanted to ruin the fun they'd been having. The only time they were along during the trip had pretty much been when they were in bed together, and talk about a buzz kill that would've been.

And since they'd gotten home, they hadn't been alone together for more than a handful of minutes. They'd gone right back to their normal routine, where their paths only crossed at dinner, if that. Once again, it seemed like he was avoiding her. She wasn't sure what hurt more, being kicked out of his bed or him not even talking to her about it.

"I just… I feel like I'm being stupid. He's a freaking billionaire for god's sake. Why would he be interested in more than just a vacation fling with me?" Trisha sighed and fought back the tears welling up inside her. She'd been having these thoughts for a while now, but this was the first time she'd vocalized them. "I'm just the hired help."

Sam pulled her into a hug. "Oh, honey. You're more than just 'hired help.' You're smart and gorgeous and stronger than any other woman I know. He's lucky to have you there. And if he's too stupid to realize that, then you deserve better. Don't waste your time on a man who has his head too far up his ass to see how lucky he really is."

Trisha snorted. Leave it to Sam to know just what to say to make her feel better.

She was right though. Just because he didn't think she was worth more than a few nights in bed didn't mean it was true. She was at the top of all of her classes. She was close to graduating with a degree from a prestigious university. Why should she have to settle for a man who barely noticed her, even if he was handsome and rich?

Once Trisha regained her composure, the two of them went out for a girls' night. It was late by the time she headed home, but she felt much better than before. She'd barely thought about Jonathan the entire night, letting the boys on the dance floor occupy her mind for a few hours.

But when she walked in the front door of Ashcourt Manor, all the progress she'd made disappeared. Jonathan was just come down the steps, wearing nothing but a pair of pajama bottoms, his toned torso bare.

Each and every contour of his muscles was ingrained in Trisha's mind. She'd spent hours just letting her hands roam across his body, soaking it all in. He had a body most men could only dream of, a body she dreamt of frequently.

If she closed her eyes, she could see the droplets of water sliding down his torso as they showered. She could see him glistening with sweat in the moonlight. She could see up atop her as they made love to each other.

She could remember each and every moment they'd shared in Italy.

She froze and stared, all the wheels in her mind grinding to a halt. She couldn't tear her eyes away from him, couldn't stop her heart from pounding as she recalled the last few times she'd seen him like that. Already a fire began to stir inside her, one she couldn't quell no matter how hard she tried.

"Welcome back," he said with a smile. His voice was rich and velvety smooth. Even after she'd dismissed her feelings for him, he still made her shiver with just a few words. "Did you have fun with your friends?"

Trisha nodded, unable to speak. It was all she could do not to run and jump into his arms and press her lips to his. But this wasn't a movie, and he wasn't her Prince Charming. He was her boss, a man she'd allowed herself a little fun with, but that was over now. She needed to get her mind back on track, get used to just being his nanny once again.

That was, until Jonathan moved to stand only inches from her. She swallowed the lump in her throat as she looked up into his eyes. God... those eyes. Just a look from him had her throwing caution to the wind, ignoring everything she'd decided earlier.

She could smell the minty soap he always used. This close, she could almost taste him again. Her heart hammered faster and faster until she thought she might have a heart attack. It was all she could do to keep her wobbly knees from collapsing beneath her.

"I've missed you," Jonathan said, wrapping his arms around her and pulling them tight together. When he leaned down and pressed his lips to hers, she didn't fight it. Instead, she kissed him right back. All those thoughts of things going back to normal had fled like they were never there. "Care to join me in my room tonight?"

Trisha nodded. Her voice still refused to work. Her brain barely even functioned for that matter. But she couldn't say no to him. No matter how much that tiny voice in the back of her head told her not to do this, she didn't stop him when he led her back up the stairs.

She'd been dreaming of this since they'd gotten back from Italy. Hell, she'd been dreaming of this since the day she'd moved into Ashcourt Manor. She couldn't count the number of times she'd thought about him sweeping her of her feet and taking her up to his room to have his way with her.

This wasn't exactly being swept off her feet, but it was a close second!

The moment they were in his bedroom, her eyes went wide. It was as if she was visiting the house for the very first time again, stunned by its elegance and beauty.

Her room paled in comparison to his. It was massive, with ornate furniture and woodwork everywhere. The curtains and carpet were a deep, velvety red. All the trim was done in gold. The bed in the center was larger than any she'd ever seen before.

The room looked like it housed royalty. She'd only every seen rooms like this in magazines or on the internet. And yet, somehow, it fit Jonathan.

There were personal touched all over. Picture frames adorned the dresser. Photographs hung on the wall, rather than artwork. Trisha wandered around the room, looking over each one. The ones hanging on the walls were all landscapes and cityscapes, taken by an expert photographer no doubt.

But the ones on the dresser and nightstands were more personal. There were pictures of the boys, pictures of Jonathan dressed in a tux with a gorgeous woman on his arm, and even pictures of Jonathan with an older couple she assumed were his parents.

She picked up the one of Jonathan and the woman, looking it over carefully. Jonathan slipped his arms around her waist, leaning his head on her shoulder, not speaking, just allowing her the freedom to examine everything.

She had a feeling not many people ever ventured into this room. As far as she knew, even Judith rarely came in her while she cleaned the house. For all she knew, she was the first woman to have set foot in this room in many years.

"Was this your wife?" she asked quietly. She knew the answer without asking, since Declan and Alexander both had her eyes. Still, she wanted to hear what Jonathan had to say about the mysterious woman.

Jonathan nodded. "Yes. That's Jackie. It was taken at fundraising gala many years ago, before Declan was even born."

"Do you miss her?"

"Sometimes," Jonathan admitted, his voice low. "It was really hard for the first few years, but I've come to terms with everything for the most part. Having the boys really helped, since I knew I still had a part of her with me. Every time I look into their eyes, I can still see her smiling back at me."

Trisha fought back her inner psychologist. It wasn't her place to barge into Jonathan's personal thoughts. She'd already trudged into uncertain territory.

"How did the boys handle it?"

Jonathan sighed. For a moment, she wasn't sure he'd answer. She was sure he was about to send her back to her own bedroom. Then, he spoke. "Declan was only two when she died, so he barely remembers her now. It'd taken a little while for him to get used to things, but he adjusted. It was harder on Alexander, since he'd been six at the time.

"I took some time off work, to spend with the boys, so that helped. But it was hard for Alexander to under-stand why his mother wasn't coming back. It's hard to explain cancer and death to a kid that young. He insisted on sleeping with me every night for about a month. I think he was afraid I might leave him too.

"But he adjusted, eventually. Sometimes though, I'll find him in his room, holding a picture of the two of them together. But having Grace and Gretta helped, since they'd been part of the family since before he was born. I think it hurt when Grace left to move to Florida, but I think he really likes having you here. I know I do."

Trisha flushed at the compliment. At least now she knew why Alexander had been a bit distant to her, unlike Declan who'd latched onto her almost the moment she'd stepped in the door. But Alexander hadn't pushed her away either and she hadn't seen any resentment from him, just caution.

Her heart went out to both boys. Losing a parent was hard on anyone, but especially on a child. It was a wound that never healed completely. She was glad the boy hadn't completely rejected her and instead seemed to enjoy her company when they spent the nights playing video games together or doing homework together.

Maybe it was because Trisha was so young, she thought. He probably sees her as more of an older sister type figure, rather than as a replacement for his mother. She'd never be able to replace their mother, not for Alexander and not for Declan or Jonathan.

After setting the picture back where it has been, she turned in Jonathan's arms and wrapped her own arms around his waist. She could see sadness in his eyes, but he made no move to send her away. Instead, they just gazed at each other, neither sure what to do next.

Finally, Trisha spoke. "We don't have to do this, if you don't want to."

In response, Jonathan leaned down and kissed her firmly. Just that quick kiss had her heartrate spiking again, her knees going weak.

"I want to. More than anything."

When Jonathan pulled her toward the bed, Trisha didn't fight. She crawled into bed next to him, his arms once against around her and pulling them tight. As they kissed, his hands slid beneath her shirt, gently caressing her back.

It didn't take long before Trisha's shirt and bra were in a pile on the floor. The fire that had been building up inside her sprung to life as their bare chests pressed together. All rational thoughts left her mind as Jonathan continued to run his fingers over her body. She couldn't wait to feel him inside her again.

Trisha straddled Jonathan's hips, his cock already hard

and pressing against her. Even with both of them still wearing pants, she could feel his bulge as he lifted his hips off the bed and ground against her. When Trisha broke the kiss and grinned down at him, he grinned back.

Moments later, their pants and underwear were on the ground as well and they were back to kissing. Trisha was already wet, just from Jonathan touching and kissing her. He really did know how to push all of her buttons. And she knew, if she let him, he'd spend all day making her scream in pleasure.

But this time, she was going to be the one in control.

She took hold of his wrists and pinned them above his head, not breaking the kiss. Then she started grinding against his hard cock. He'd spent their week in Italy teasing her and making her beg for more. Now it was time for a little bit of revenge.

If only she had some straps to tie him to the bed, she thought. Oh the fun she could have with him completely helpless and in her control… She doubted he ever relinquished control to anyone, so she was going to enjoy every moment of this.

She broke the kiss and grinned down at him. "Keep your hands there," she said, then release her grin. Once she was sure he wouldn't move, Trisha took a page out of his book and began kissing down his body.

The man truly was sculpted by the gods. Her body quivered as she ran her lips and tongue over his muscles, tracing each one until he began to shiver under her touch. He'd spent so much time teasing and torturing her, and she was going to enjoy every second of returning that pleasure to him.

When she reached his cock, she ignored it completely, instead kissing down one leg and up the other. Even as she worked her way back up his body, she still didn't pay any attention to his throbbing member. She was able to come a few times in one night, but he wasn't, not without a bit of rest, so she had to hold herself back just a bit.

The last thing she needed was for him to come and go limp. She had far too much planned for that to happen. So she focused on touch and kissing and licking every other part of his body until his light moans bounced off the walls around them. The more she worked on his body, the louder his moans became.

And here, they didn't have to worry about being quiet. Jonathan's room was on the third floor, with the boys being sound asleep on the floor below them. There was no way they'd hear anything tonight. Which meant neither of them had to hold back.

More than once, Jonathan tried to lift his hips and grind his cock against Trisha, but she wasn't having any of that. Each time he moved, he earned a light smack on the thigh. He pouted at her, but all she did was smirk in response.

Her entire body tingled as she teased Jonathan. The only downside to delaying the pleasure for him was that she had to delay her own pleasure. Part of he wanted to just impale herself on his thick cock and ride him until he exploded.

But another part of her knew that wasn't the right course of action. She couldn't give in to his temptations, no matter how much she wanted to. He needed to get a taste of his own medicine, needed to see what it was like to beg before you were given release.

"Oh fuck!" Jonathan yelled out as Trisha began to nibble on his neck. He arched his hips again, earning him another smack. Trisha waited until he'd calmed down slightly before she went back to her task at hand.

Each time Jonathan seemed to approach the edge, Trisha would back off, grinning as he glared at her.

This was definitely something he wasn't used to, which just made it even better.

Trisha lost track of how long it'd been since they'd started. Jonathan's cock looked harder than ever, coated in his own precum from his excitement. Trisha licked her lips, fighting to keep from licking the delectable seed from his cock.

But she knew if she did that, he wouldn't be able to hold back any longer.

When she saw his hands ball into fists, Trisha grinned. His entire body was flushed now, his cock twitching every couple seconds. The head of his cock was red, just begging for relief now. It wouldn't be long before Jonathan begged her to ride him.

She started kissing along his jaw line, letting her hands roam across his chest. With each passing second, his breathing became more and more shallow. She was sure his heart had to be hammering in his chest as well.

"Please…. Trisha…" Jonathan gritted his teeth, his eyes burning with lust now. She was actually surprised he had kept his hands above his head and hadn't just lifted her and rolled her over.

"You sure you're ready for this?" she asked, batting her eyes at him. "You sure you don't need a little break?"

Now Jonathan growled, grabbing her hips and thrusting up to rub his cock against her dripping pussy. "What do you think?"

*I think* I'm *about to come*, her inner voice shouted. She didn't have much choice but to give into his pleading. She was going to drive herself nuts if she waited much longer!

She lifted her hips and reached between them to grasp his cock. Jonathan sucked in a breath at the contact, making Trisha grin again. Well, at least she wasn't the only one about ready to explode! When she moved his cock to line up with her entrance, she had to take a deep breath to calm herself.

And when she finally lowered herself onto Jonathan's cock, both of them moaned out. There was no way either of them were going to last very long. She was a bit too good at her foreplay this time. Oh well. Maybe they'd cuddle for a bit and go for round two after!

For a few moments, neither one moved. Both tried desperately to control their breathing, to keep their bodies under control. She'd done her job a little two well, and both of them were right on the verge of coming.

"Ready?" Trisha asked. When Jonathan nodded, she leaned forward and kissed him. As their tongues dueled, she began rocking her hips back and forth, fucking herself on his cock.

It didn't take long before his hands were at her waist, his fingers digging into her. He started to lift off the bed, thrusting against her as she continued to rock. They built into a rhythm together as they moaned into each other's mouths.

This was the perfect way to muffle their sounds of pleasure, Trisha thought to herself. Though tonight, they didn't have to be careful. The boys weren't right across a tiny living room from them. This house had been built well, sound not traveling far at all.

Tonight, they could let loose.

Trisha broke the kiss and moaned openly. "Oh god. Fuck me, Jonathan. Fuck me!"

The two of them moved faster now, both desperately chasing their own orgasms. Jonathan's breathing came in grunt. His lust filled eyes looked up at her, and she knew she could easily spend hours in his bed, riding him like a bull.

That wasn't meant to be though, as fire coursed through her veins. A storm raged inside her, lashing out every few seconds, telling her just how close to the end she was. Already, stars began to swim in front of her eyes.

"Gonna come…" she breathed out between her gritted teeth. She wanted to hold on, but nothing would be able to prolong the inevitable for long.

Jonathan began to thrust faster now. Trisha bent over, bracing herself with her forearms on both sides of Jonathan's head. As she looked into his eyes and saw the pure lust reflected back at her, she lost control.

Her voice echoed off the walls. Her entire body shook and shivered. All of reality seemed to be distorted. The only sensations she was able to focus on was Jonathan's cock still pistoning in and out of her cunt. Everything else vanished from her perception as immense pleasure flooded her body.

Her pussy clamped down onto Jonathan's cock like a vice. He only lasted a moment or two longer before his groan of pleasure mingled with hers. He thrust up into her again just as he cock throbbed. A shockwave rippled through her body as he filled her with his cum.

Trisha gasped for air. Her heart seemed ready to leap from her chest. God, it seemed like no matter how many times she had sex with Jonathan, each time was better than the last. She couldn't even move off of him right away, her head still foggy.

By the time she rolled off, she was acutely aware of her exhaustion. She'd completely lost track of time, but she knew it had gotten late, even without looking at the clock. The room smelled of sweat and cum already

When Jonathan put his arm around Trisha, she snuggled against him. Part of her wanted to go shower and wash off, but the rest of her knew there was no chance in hell of that happening. Which is why, before she knew it, she was sound asleep, her head resting on Jonathan's chest.

## ❧ 20 ❧

## JONATHAN

*BEEP BEEP BEEP*

Groggily, Jonathan swatted at his alarm clock until the incessant beeping stopped. As the fog in his mind slowly dissipated, he realized he wasn't alone in bed. He turned to see Trisha laying against his side, still sleeping.

For a moment, his heart came to a stop. He'd never had a woman in here since Jackie had died. No one other than the boys really every came up here. To wake up in his bed with a woman laying right next to him was a complete shock. It took him a moment before he was sure he was awake and not just dreaming.

Then, memories of last night came back, and he grinned up at the ceiling. He was glad he'd brought Trisha up here last night. He was glad he'd opened himself up to her once again. Sure, he was going to be tired in the office today, but it was nothing some coffee couldn't take care of. Last night he'd let Trisha take control of their sex, and she hadn't disappointed him in the least!

Damn, that woman knew what she was doing.

As he looked down at her naked body, barely covered by the blanket, he considered waking her up for another round. Then he decided against it. She would need her strength for taking care of the boys today. Since the boys wouldn't be awake until closer to noon, there was no reason to wake her up just as the sun was rising.

Carefully, Jonathan slid out of bed. Then he pulled the blankets up to cover Trisha again while he headed to the bathroom. A hot shower went a long way toward waking him up. As the water washed away the dried sweat from last night, his muscles began to loosen up.

Even if he had only gotten a few hours of sleep, he'd still slept like the dead. He'd had worse nights of sleep, that was for sure.

He still couldn't believe he'd managed to go three times last night without an effort. If he hadn't been exhausted by the end of round three, he probably could've gone for a forth. It was like he was a randy teenager again, able to get it up at the drop of a hat.

Damn, Trisha really did have some effect on him.

And it wasn't just sex either. He could've gone back to her room and fucked her there if he'd wanted to. Yet, when he'd held her downstairs, he didn't even consider that. He wanted to bring her upstairs with him, to take her to his room, to lie in his bed with her in his arms.

When he went back into the bedroom, freshly show-ered and shaved, Trisha was still sound asleep beneath his blanket. For a few moments, he stood and watched her sleep, his heart swelling. It'd been a long time since he'd had anyone in his bed. He'd started to think he'd never have another woman in his bed ever again.

He'd slept with women since his wife had died, but he'd never brought them back to his room though. He still wasn't quite sure why he'd asked Trisha to come up with him last night, but he was glad he did. She looked right at home in his California King bed.

If he had his way, she'd be spending an awful lot of nights there.

There was still a lot he wanted to learn about Trisha's body. He wasn't going to stop until he knew every single inch of her. He'd been exploring her body quite a bit, but every time they'd had sex, it was always hot and heavy, leaving both of them gasping for air by the time they finished.

Even last night, with Trisha spending god knows how long kissing and licking his body, she'd had to be careful not to set him off with her teasing. Just as he wanted to know all of the buttons to press to keep her right on the edge, he wanted her to learn all his buttons as well.

They both had much to learn.

And Jonathan was looking forward to those lessons!

By the time he'd dressed, the sun's rays had begun to fill the room. As he stood in the doorway, gazing at Trisha again, he had to fight back the urge to walk over there and kiss her. In the end, he left the room, shutting the door quietly to keep from disturbing her.

Kissing her like that would bring things to a whole new level, one he wasn't quite sure he was ready for. Sure, they'd made out, but that was just another part of their foreplay. It wasn't the long, sensual kisses or even the light, fluttery kisses he'd shared all those years ago.

He quite enjoyed having Trisha in his bed at night, but that was where he planned to keep things for now. It was one thing for them to enjoy their mutual lust in the privacy of the bedroom, but that was where it needed to stay. The boys, Alexander in particular, were liable to throw a fit if he pursued a relationship with Trisha.

Even if a deep part of his mind told him it was time to move on, to leave the past in the past, he couldn't bring himself to do it. It wouldn't be fair to the kids to bring another woman into the house permanently. It wouldn't be fair to replace their mother like that, even though he knew no one would ever be able to replace Jackie.

By the time he got to his office, his heart was still heavy in his chest. He tried to push all the thoughts of Trisha away, but no matter how hard he tried, he just couldn't. A hot cup of coffee from the café down the street helped, but it still wasn't enough to completely banish his personal thoughts.

Carla wasn't in yet, which gave him a little bit more peace and quiet as he started going over the leftover paperwork from Friday. That was the downside to his job. The paperwork never seemed to have an end. He could only imagine how many trees they killed in just this building alone.

Luckily, he had meeting scheduled for most of the day.

That'd help keep him from thinking about Trisha, for a few hours at least.

"Good morning!" Carla said, as bubbly as ever. How that woman managed to be so perky and alive first thing in the morning, Jonathan would never know. He suspected a caffeine IV but had yet to confirm that.

"Morning," he said, looking away from his computer. He eyed the stack of papers in her arms, frowning as she approached. "Don't tell me those are all for me."

He groaned when she grinned at him. She set the stack down in front of him, still looking like the cat that ate the canary. "These just came up. It's the final plans for next month's gala. Everything seems to be in order, it just all needs your final approval."

"You know how much I just love paperwork first thing in the morning." Jonathan sighed and began thumbing through the stack. "When do they need this back by?"

"Tomorrow."

Now Jonathan groaned even louder. Oh how he'd missed being out in Italy. Being in meetings all day with people who barely seemed to speak English was much preferable to paperwork. Now he'd have to juggle paperwork *and* his meetings. What was the point of having people working for him if he still had to go over everything himself?

So much for having a lunch break.

"Have one of the interns bring me a sub for lunch, will you? It looks like I'm going to be stuck here all day." That was one of the perks of being at the top of the company. There was never a shortage of grunts willing to run errands.

"Your usual?" When Jonathan nodded, she scribbled something onto her pad. That was the good thing about Carla. She knew him better than almost anyone at the company. "Anything else?"

"Can you schedule a meeting with Christopher Sellock sometime this week? I want to sit down and review all the architectural plans and see how they're coming along." Jonathan rattled off a few other things he needed her to take care of or check into.

Once she was gone, he dove head first into the paperwork for the gala. That had to be done first, since they were running on a tight deadline. There were contracts for the caters that needed signing, budgets approved for the decorations, and a thousand other minute details. You'd never think one little event needed that much planning until you started. Thankfully, this wasn't his first rodeo, so he was able to get through most of it without issue.

"Having fun?" A deep voice said. He'd been so absorbed in the paperwork he'd jumped a bit at the sound. When he looked up, he saw Timothy Erickson, his VP, leaning against the doorframe, grinning at him.

The man was tall and slender, bordering on lanky and looking every bit the geek he'd been in college. No matter how many expensive suits or designer glasses you gave the guy, he still looked like your typical nerd, which always made Jonathan smile. Some things just never changed, thankfully.

Jonathan pursed his lips. "You know how much I just love paperwork. Why do I have to sign off on all this anyway? Isn't that what I pay you guys to do?"

Timothy chuckled and walked in, plopping down in the chair across from him. The two of them had been friends since college, starting the company together. Jonathan had been the dreamer, while Timothy had been the one who knew how to make those dreams a reality. In the early days, Jonathan had handled the business aspects and was their original source of capital, while Timothy had been the one slaving away in his basement workshop.

Now Jonathan was head of a multi-billion dollar corporation and Timothy ran their entire R&D department. Jonathan had thought the arrangement was a bit lopsided, but Timothy always said he was more comfortable dealing with machines and other scientists, rather than the ass kissing required to be CEO.

"You know how things are. No one wants to be responsible if something gets screwed up. And this is a big function. Everything needs to go off without a hitch so we can impress the investors. Plus, there will be media folks all over the place."

Jonathan sighed and nodded. Timothy always was his voice of reason. And he usually was right. This gala had to go off without a hitch if he wanted to secure the investors he needed. He'd come too far to let things fall apart because the caterer never got their contract signed. The few investors he'd already gotten wouldn't be enough to fully realize his dreams. Which meant he just needed to suck it up and deal with the paperwork.

"So what brings you up here?" Jonathan asked as he turned his focus back to the seemingly endless stack of papers. If he wanted to get them done soon, he'd have to work and talk at the same time, even if he really wanted to just sit and chat with his old friend. "You rarely venture out of your little lab downstairs."

"The board sent one of their little paper-pushers down to ask me to today's meeting." He frowned. Meetings with the board were Jonathan's specialty. But to Timothy, they were an endless cycle of anxiety. It was another reason Jonathan ran the company while Timothy made sure all the tech worked. "They want to talk about the MediPads apparently."

The MediPads were Timothy's current project. He'd been working on them fulltime for over a year now. They were tablets designed specifically for use in hospitals and doctor's offices. Timothy was heading everything up, overseeing the hardware and software needed to revolutionize medicine.

Doctors and nurses would've have to worry about paper charts and files. They wouldn't have to worry about physical X-rays or test results. They'd be able to access all of their patient's information on their Medi-Pad. They'd be able to transmit files to other doctors for consultations or referrals. Best of all, the custom hardware would be able to withstand the heavy use in a hospital environment. They'd be sturdy enough to withstand being dropped or things being spilled on them. But they'd be easy enough to sanitize as well.

It'd been something Jonathan had thought of years ago,

back when they were still in school. It'd been a side-project of Timothy's since then. Now that side project was finally coming to light. He'd produced a prototype last year and was working on refining everything now.

It was supposed to be one of the main selling points of the hospital they were building. Everything in the hospital would be connected and accessible through the MediPads. Any information the doctors or nurses needed would be right at their fingertips.

That is, as long as the board doesn't decide to pull the plug on the project. Jonathan knew they'd be stupid to do so. Not only would the project revolutionize the way doctors handled patient records, but it'd bring in a fortune for the company.

But the board were a bunch of old farts with old money. They weren't big on things that were risky ventures, which the MediPad was. The device relied on becoming an industry standard. It wouldn't succeed unless it had near universal adoption.

"Relax," Jonathan told him, smiling. "I'm sure they just want a status update on how everything is going. I haven't heard any rumblings, so I doubt they're going to do anything drastic. Besides, if we don't release the

MediPad, someone else will. It's only a matter of time with how digital society is becoming."

Timothy nodded, but didn't relax at all. "I guess it's a good thing we've been making progress then. All that's left really is working out some of the software bugs before it's ready to go into production."

"Good. Then the board can't complain. Although, I'm sure they will. You know how those old farts are. If they can't complain about anything, they complain about not being able to complain."

Jonathan grinned at him, hoping to put Timothy at ease a little. He doubted the board would pull the plug after this much work had gone into it, but you never did know with that group of old fogeys. Not everyone was keen on change nor did they always trust technology.

Before he knew it, it was time for the two of them to head down to the meeting with the board. Just as he'd suspected, they wanted a status update on the Medi-Pads. Timothy may have been a nervous ball of energy, but he was passionate about his projects, which helped ease the old fogey's minds.

Everything was on track for their December launch of the project. The hardware was stable and ready for production. All that was left were a few bugs in the coding and the tablets would be ready for production. They'd be given to a few local doctors to test out before the hospital opened, this way they'd have actual field experience before the hospital was even finished being built.

The last thing they needed was for some major snafu to pop up that would cripple the hospital. Which was why they planned on testing small batches at first in less critical environments before the hospital was even finished being built. They'd thought of every contingency, at least Jonathan hoped they had.

T risha stared at herself in Jonathan's bathroom mirror. Just like the rest of his room, it was ornate and gilded and prob ably cost more than she had in her bank account. Jonathan had left for work an hour ago. She'd feigned sleep, not quite ready to face the day. Not quite ready to face *him*.

Even though he'd left without waking her most mornings, it was different than it had been that first night. She didn't feel abandoned or that he'd snuck out. Instead, it felt almost natural, like he was being considerate by not waking her at dawn when he left, letting her sleep in until it was time to start taking care of the boys.

Things had been going well since their trip to Italy.

Even though she'd been a little iffy for a few days after they'd returned, once Jonathan had taken her to bed, she'd slept with him every night since. They fucked at least twice before falling asleep in each other's arms.

He'd been coming home for dinner almost every single night, something the boys were very happy about. The four of them would eat together, then either play video games or watch a movie until it was time for the boys to head to sleep. Then, it would just be the two of them, and they'd head up to Jonathan's bedroom.

Everything seemed to be perfect, until last night. After they'd had sex and cuddled together under the blankets, Jonathan had fallen asleep almost right away. She couldn't really blame him, since he was getting up near dawn every morning to head into work and staying there until almost dinner time.

But as she'd lain staring up at the ceiling, Jonathan's arm draped across her stomach, she realized something. It'd been well over a month since she'd gotten her last period. She should've gotten it last week, but it hadn't come.

She'd slept fitfully all night as she considered the possibilities. She'd never had a late period before. Her schedule was always regular, even more so than any other woman she'd met. And since she'd never even thought to use condoms, that left only one possibility.

She was pregnant.

It was stupid, she told herself as she started at her reflection. Why hadn't they used protection? She wasn't on the pill, since it didn't agree with her body and made her sick. She should've insisted on them using condoms, especially after their first night together.

Yet, each time she'd fallen into Jonathan's arms, the only thing that had been on her mind was feeling his cock inside her. Once they'd gotten going, birth control was the furthest thing from her mind.

Now what was she going to do?

She needed to get a pregnancy test done, but was scared of what the results might say. Worse, she was scared of what Jonathan might say if she really was pregnant. Would he throw her out and pretend he didn't know her anymore? Would he insist on her having an abortion?

She shivered at the thought. There was no way she was getting an abortion. It didn't matter that she still had at least one more year of school left. It didn't matter if Jonathan tossed her out on her own. This baby would be part of her, and she wasn't going to give it up, not without a fight.

Before the boys woke up, she called Sam and made plans to meet with her at the park. She needed to get out of the house and talk to someone, but she couldn't leave the boys home alone. The park seemed like a good place for those two to occupy themselves while Sam and Trisha had a private chat.

A few hours later, Sam and Trisha were sitting beneath the sun's rays as they watched Declan and Alexander toss a football. Trisha's heart hammered in her chest as she thought about that to say to Sam.

This wasn't going to be an easy chat.

"So, did you bring me here to talk about something or just to watch the boys play football?" Sam looked side-eyed at her. "'Cause, I have to tell you, as entertaining as this is, neither of those boys are ever going to go pro."

Trisha snorted. Just as Sam said the words, Declan dove for the ball, missed, and came up with dirt all over his pants. There was definitely a reason they preferred video games over sports most of the time! But hey, they were having fun and that was all that mattered. Plus, they were distracted for a little while, giving her and Sam a chance to talk.

"Talk. Definitely talk," Trisha said. She took a deep breath and closed her eyes. How should she broach the subject?

"Just spit it out."

That was Sam, never one for beating around the bush. But, like always, she was right. There wasn't much point in cherry coating it or delaying the inevitable. She just needed to come out and say what was on her mind.

"I think I'm pregnant."

Sam's head whirled around so fast Trisha thought she might've given herself whiplash. Sam stared at her. Her mouth opened and closed a few times, making Trisha giggle. This was the first time she'd ever seen Sam speechless.

"W..What? How?" Sam waved a hand. "Never mind, I know how. Is it Jonathans?"

Trisha nodded, her face flushing. She'd never felt like this before. Guilt and shame washed over her, even though she had no reason for it. She was an adult, perfectly capable of having sex and children. So why did she feel like this?

And yet, she couldn't shake it. She'd known better than to have sex without protection yet had done it anyway. What was Jonathan going to say when he found out? When she hadn't insisted on a condom, he probably assumed she was on the pill or something.

Samantha wrapped her arms around Trisha and hugged her tight. Trisha gasped as the air was forced from her lungs. Then she patted Sam gently on the back before pushing her away. Well, at least someone was excited.

"Oh my god! This is amazing news!" Sam bounced up and down, grinning like a madman now. "Do the boys know yet?"

Trisha shook her head, the flush in her cheeks deepening. "I haven't even told Jonathan…"

"Why not? He's going to be so excited! I can't wait to throw you a baby shower. I wonder if it'll be a boy or a girl…."

"What if he doesn't want me to keep it?"

Sam froze, her eyebrows rising. "Why wouldn't he? I thought you said things were going good between the two of you."

Trisha shrugged. Things had been going pretty well. At

least, they weren't horrible. But Trisha was still essentially his mistress, their relationship being confined to the bedroom. She had a feeling Jonathan wanted it that way.

He barely spoke about his late wife, but he didn't seem to be in any hurry to marry again. As far as she had gleamed over the past few months, he hadn't dated anyone since she'd died. So why would he make an exception for her?

It wasn't like she was anything special. She was just the girl he'd fallen into bed with. Now she was the *pregnant* girl he'd fallen into bed with. Not to mention she was his nanny! This whole thing had Jerry Springer written all over it.

Boy, didn't she know how to pick them?

"Things haven't been bad," Trisha said at least. "But it's really just been sex between the two of us. We've never gone on a date. We haven't even really been out of the house together since Italy. And it's not like he's told the boys about us."

Sam kept an arm around Trisha and leaned her head on Trisha's shoulder. Even without saying anything, Trisha relaxed a bit from the contact with Sam. "You should talk to him. Sit down and tell him how you feel. This is gonna be his kid, too. He deserves to know."

Just once, Trisha wanted Sam to be wrong about something. One person had no right to be correct all the time. But she couldn't deny what Sam said was true. She did need to talk to him, the question was how?

He'd been extremely busy over the past few days, what with his company working on building that new hospital and the charity ball that was coming up. When he'd first mentioned it at dinner one night, Trisha had a small hope he might invite her to go with him, but she'd already given up that little fantasy.

Sam and Trisha spent a little while longer talking until the boys seemed to wear themselves out. After getting them some food, Sam went back to her apartment, giving Trisha a hug and some words of encouragement. Trisha wasn't sure what she'd do without a friend like Sam.

She decided to wait a few days until she could take a pregnancy test and be completely sure. Then, she'd pull Jonathan aside when the boys were busy and talk to him. Then, she'd tell him the truth and hope for the best.

What else could she do?

## 22

### JONATHAN

"So, who are you bringing to the gala next week?" Timothy asked. He sat in one of the chairs in front of Jonathan's desk, hands behind his head, relaxing like he didn't have a care in the world.

Jonathan scowled at him. He just had to bring up his date. Most of the time he went with a friend or a coworker, at least he had since Jackie had passed away. But this year he wasn't quite sure what to do.

He'd thought about bringing Trisha, but he still wasn't sure if he wanted to make that step yet. She'd spent every night for the last week in his bed, and he his attraction to her grew with each passing day. But was he ready to make things official with her?

"I'm not sure yet."

"You should bring Trisha," he said, like he'd been reading Jonathan's mind. Damn him for knowing Jonathan so well. "She sounds like a lovely person. I'm sure she'd have fun."

Except he didn't know what was going on between the two of them. If they'd just been friends or if she'd still just been his nanny, he wouldn't have hesitated to invite her to be his date for the evening. But with how things had been going between them, if he asked her to be his date for the night, it wouldn't be just platonic.

"Maybe," Jonathan said. He wasn't quite ready to commit to anything yet.

Part of him screamed to just do it. To just ask Trisha to take the next step with him. And yet, another part of him wanted to push her away all together before things got too serious. The last thing he needed was for the boys to get even more emotionally invested in her, then have them break up. It would devastate both of them.

And, above everything else, he was a father first. He couldn't risk doing anything that would upset the boys. Even if it meant being single for the rest of his life, he wouldn't do anything that would hurt them. Their needs came before his.

Yet, even after Timothy went back down to his lab, all

Jonathan could do was think about what he'd said. Should he ask Trisha to attend the charity gala with him? Like Timothy said, he was sure she'd have fun there. It'd get her out of the house and away from the boys for the night, too.

Maybe he could talk to her, make sure she understood that she'd just be there as his friend.

But that wouldn't be fair to her.

He'd basically be telling her he didn't want anyone to know about their relationship, that he was ashamed of her or something. If he did that, he'd completely ruin any chances of ever making this more than just casual sex between the two of them. Hell, he'd be lucky if she didn't storm out and never speak to him again.

At the same time, he still wasn't sure if he wanted this to be more than just casual sex. No, that wasn't true. He *knew* he wanted more out of this relationship. But he wasn't sure if he should take the next step. Things just weren't that simple in his life, not with two boys to take into consideration.

He needed to make sure this absolutely the best step to take before he did anything.

By the time he headed home for the evening, he still

hadn't made up his mind. Dinner was excruciating that night, since every time he made eye contact with Trisha, his stomach tossed and turned. He needed to make up his mind and soon.

After the boys were asleep, Trisha came up to his room again. Despite his mind still being in turmoil, he couldn't help but grin as she slipped inside. No matter how confused or upset he was, Trisha never failed to make him smile.

To make him happy.

And, as it turned out, she knew just the way to distract him from his thoughts for an hour or two. Once she slipped out of her clothes and crawled into his bed, all thoughts disappeared from his mind. His only focus was on Trisha.

It wasn't until she'd fallen asleep, curled up against his side, his arm around her shoulders, that his thoughts returned. As he stared up at the ceiling, his mind was much clearer than it had been that morning. With Trisha breathing softly beside him, he knew what he wanted now.

He wanted Trisha.

He *needed* Trisha.

WHEN TRISHA DISAPPEARED ON SUNDAY TO GO VISIT her friends, Jonathan found the boys sitting in the game room. He was pretty sure they spent more time in there than in their actual bedrooms, but if they were keeping out of trouble, he couldn't really complain.

"You guys got a minute?" he asked, sitting on the couch's armrest.

He waited until they were able to pause the game, then turned to face them. As they looked up at him expectantly, Jonathan's heart began to pound. He'd negotiated deals worth millions of dollars, yet none of that had made him as nervous as he was right now.

It was amazing the affect two small boys had on him. What they said today would determine a big part of his future.

"What do you guys think of Trisha?" he asked. That seemed like a safe way to start the conversation. Still though, his heart pounded as he waited for their answers.

Alexander shrugged. He frowned though, his brow coming together. He knew there was more to the question. "She's okay, I guess."

"I like her! She's cool!" Declan said, grinning broadly. Clearly he was much happier with his new nanny than his older brother was. But then, Declan was younger and more open to changes.

Well, that was a start, he figured. He was pretty sure Alexander liked her a bit more than he was letting on. He'd gotten to that stage recently where he feigned indifference to everything. But if Jonathan didn't tread carefully, Alexander would fight every step of the way.

"Do you guys like having her around?"

Declan nodded eagerly, while Alexander gave a single nod.

Well, it was now or never, he figured. There wasn't much point in beating around the bush any more. Might as well get it over with before he lost their attention. Neither boy was known for their long attention span.

He took a deep breath and tried to smile, though he knew it probably looked as fake as it felt. "What would you think if I asked Trisha out on a date?"

Both boys stared at him now. Declan furrowed his brow. Alexander's frown deepened. Neither boy seemed to know quite what to think.

"Would that make her our new mom?" Declan asked quietly, making Alexander scowl.

Jonathan ruffled the boy's hair. "No, not necessarily. She would be my girlfriend and still be your nanny. I really like her, but if you two aren't okay with us dating, then we won't. It's up to you."

Alexander was the first to respond. He shrugged and picked up his game controller again. "I don't care."

There was that feigned indifference again. Jonathan was pretty sure he cared more than he let on, but he let it sit for now. When Alex was ready to talk, he'd talk. Until then, there wasn't much point in pressing things. And hey, at least he hadn't completely dismissed the idea! That was a good thing, right?

Declan looked between his brother and Jonathan, his little brow still furrowed. Jonathan could practically see the wheels turning in his head as he thought about everything. Then, finally, he nodded. "I guess it's okay. I like Trisha. She's nice and she plays video games and stuff with us!"

Well, apparently it wasn't very hard to impress Declan. Alexander may have still been on the fence about things, but at least Declan seemed to be okay with everything. That was a step in the right direction at least. Besides, if Alexander changed his mind down the road, it wasn't like he couldn't break things off. It wasn't like they were getting married.

At least not yet.

The boys were already in bed when Trisha came home that night. And, surprisingly, she didn't come up to his room. He waited for a little while, then drifted off to sleep. When he went to work the next morning, her bedroom door was still firmly shut.

Jonathan just shrugged as he made himself some coffee. She must've worn herself out last night. And it wasn't like they *had* to spend every single night together. They weren't even dating, at least not yet.

But Jonathan planned to change that. After talking with the boys, he'd decided to ask her to the gala tonight. When he went into work, he had a grin on his face. Even the mountain of paperwork on his desk couldn't ruin his good mood. Not today.

He cut out of work a bit early, much to Carla's surprise, and decided to go shopping. He wanted to be prepared for tonight. Everything had to be perfect. If he wanted to ask Trisha to the gala, he wanted to be sure she'd say yes.

He slipped quietly into the house, careful not to alert anyone's attention as he snuck up to his bedroom and laid out everything he'd bought. Then he changed out of his work clothes and headed back downstairs to the dining room. Gretta was just putting dinner out when he slipped into his chair.

"Just in time," Gretta said, her lips pursed tight. She hated when he missed dinner. If she had her way, he'd be home for every single meal. Hell, if he had his way, he'd be home for every meal. Gretta's food tasted way better than any takeout lunch ever could!

"Sorry, I had to take care of a few things." He winked at her. "But you know how much I hate to miss your delicious food!"

"Mhm…" Gretta was obviously not convinced.

Jonathan had long grown used to her teasing by now. It'd become tradition at this point. Things just wouldn't be the same if he didn't have Gretta nagging him about missing her meals. Besides, it wasn't like he missed her meals intentionally. They *were* delicious after all.

Dinner was a quiet affair, except for Declan who droned on about something or another. Just as he'd gotten used to Gretta's treatment, everyone had gotten used to Declan dominating all conversations. Most nights it was more like he was having a conversation with himself. All in all, it was a pretty normal night.

Jonathan noticed Trisha didn't seem to be in a chipper mood though. She'd catch his eye, then look away. He wondered if something had happened with her friends last night and made a mental note to ask her after dinner. He figured that would be better than asking while the boys were here. He didn't want to bring up anything that might be sensitive with the boys around.

Alexander kept eyeing him as well, though at least he knew the reason for that one. Declan seemed to have moved on since their little chat yesterday, but judging by the way he kept looking between Trisha and Jonathan, he was still mulling things over. He made a mental note to talk to him, too, to help put his mind at ease.

Once they finished eating, the four of them cleaned up, then Jonathan sent the boys to go spend some time with their video games. Declan ran off without a second thought. Alexander eyed him for a moment, but when Jonathan smiled at the boy he nodded and followed his brother.

"How was your weekend off?" Jonathan asked, leaning

against the wall. He kept his eyes on Trisha, studying her.

Trisha shrugged, then sat back down at table. "It was okay. But…. Can I talk to you for a bit, while the boys are busy?"

"Sure." Jonathan pulled out a chair and sat down. His instincts had been right, it seemed. Something was going on. "Is everything okay?"

Trisha shrugged, then took a deep breath. She crossed her hands, then looked down at them. Clearly something was really bothering her. Now she had Jonathan's full attention.

"I've been thinking…." She sighed. Trisha closed her eyes for a moment, her shoulders going slack. "About us…"

Jonathan's heart sank in his chest. Just when he'd made up his mind, she was going to end things with him? He cursed himself for taking so long to make up his mind. But maybe he still had a chance…. Maybe he could still salvage things.

"What about us?" he asked, his mouth dry. He tried to swallow the lump in his throat, but it kept coming back. He had to rub his palms on his pants to dry them. God, this was so much worse than standing in front of the board. He'd rather face a bunch of old bureaucrats any day.

She sighed again. At least it seemed like this talk was as nerve-wracking for her as it was for him. Somehow, that was just a little bit comforting to him. It meant he might still have a shot and fixing things, at least he hoped he did.

"The last few weeks have been great, really they have. But…" She sighed again. "I can't keep doing this. Casual sex just isn't my thing. It's been amazing sex, really, but I need more than that from a relationship. I know that your kids have to come first and all, I get that. But if I'm going to be with a guy, I don't want it to just be in the dark, behind closed doors."

Trisha bit her lips and looked like she was on the verge of tears. Jonathan stood and offered his hand to her. Now he was sure he could fix this, at least, if he knew Trisha as well as he thought he did. "Come up to my room for a minute."

She blinked, but didn't say anything, letting Jonathan lead her upstairs. Out of the corner of his eye, he could see her brushing away the tears that threatened to fall. His heart ached to see her upset like this, and he cursed himself for having waited so long to tell her how he felt about her.

When they were outside the bedroom door, Jonathan stopped and turned to face her. "Close your eyes."

Trisha frowned, but did as he asked. Then, he led her inside carefully and closed the door behind him. He was actually surprised she'd come this far without asking him what the hell was going on.

He had a garment bag laid out on his bed, which he unzipped, though he left it closed for now. Then he picked up the bag next to it and pulled out a small box before walking back over to Trisha. "You can open your eyes now. You're not the only one who's been thinking about our relationship."

Jonathan took a deep breath. "I want things to be more than sex between us. You deserve more than that. Which is why I was hoping you would accompany me to AshCorp's charity gala next week." He opened the box and showed her the diamond necklace inside. "I was also hoping you'd wear this."

Trisha stared wide-eyed at the open box. Her mouth hung open. Jonathan grinned at her, amused at seeing how shocked she was. Apparently she hadn't been expecting him to want to stay together with her.

"It…It's gorgeous," she said at last. "I… I can't take this. It's way too expensive!"

Jonathan chuckled, then wrapped his arms around her waist. "Nothing is too expensive for you. Besides, I wouldn't want you to feel underdressed at the gala. All the woman there will be showing off the fancy things they bought with their husbands' credit cards. What kind of date would I be if I didn't make sure you looked amazing?"

"I'll have to go out and get a dress then. I don't think I own one." Trisha grinned.

He hadn't really expected her to own a dress. She'd never struck him as the dress kind of girl, which he liked about her. She didn't dress like a slob, but she also didn't spend all of her time and money on her looks. He liked how confident she was in her appearance. He liked how she dressed for comfort over style without sacrificing anything.

"I take it you'll go with me then?" When she nodded, he leaned in and kissed her. "Then you'll want this."

He led her over to the bed to where the garment bag still lay. She looked at the bag, then at him. When he nodded, she slowly opened the bag, her eyes going wide again as she looked at the sleek emerald gown that lay inside.

"Oh my god!" She ran a finger delicately over the dress. She seemed almost afraid to even touch it. Then again, it was probably the most expensive article of clothing she'd ever owned. He made a note to buy her a few more nice things to wear once in a while, even if she did prefer a t-shirt and pants.

"You can pick it up." He grinned at her.

Trisha nodded. Carefully, she picked up the dress and held it against herself. He'd chosen well, it seemed. The dress would look amazing against her caramel skin. Plus, it would match his eyes as well, letting everyone at the gala know she was with him.

It looked like he'd chosen the right size, too, judging by how it looked as she held it up against her body. "If we need to have it altered, we still have some time."

"I think it should fit," Trisha said, looking down at the dress. "It's so beautiful. Where did you get it?"

"There's a store down the street from my office. I slipped out of work a little early to get it. That's why I was almost late for dinner."

Trisha's eyes bulged again. "You don't mean Claudia's?" When Jonathan nodded, her mouth hung open. "But this had to have cost a fortune! I've seen the dresses there. They're all ungodly expensive. I've never even known someone who's gotten one of their dresses."

Jonathan plucked the dress from Trisha's hands. After carefully laying it back on the bed, he pulled her into his arms again. "I told you. I don't care how expensive it was. I just wanted something pretty for you to wear next week. I hope you like the dress."

"I love it!" she said immediately. "I've never seen anything so gorgeous." She laid her head against his chest. "Thank you, so much."

"Does that mean you don't want to break up with me anymore?"

Trisha nodded and Jonathan smiled. He was glad it hadn't been too late to salvage things between them. He wasn't sure what he'd have done if she'd still decided she'd had enough of him. But he didn't have to worry about that any more.

"What about the boys?" she asked, looked up into his eyes. "What are they going to say?"

"I've already spoken with boy of them and gotten their

approval. Both of them adore you, Declan in particular. I think Alexander is still a bit iffy on the idea, but he'll come around when he sees not much will be changing."

Trisha nodded. Then, she stood up on her toes and kissed him. "You're amazing, you know that?"

"Not nearly as amazing as you are!"

## 23

### TRISHA

Trisha's heart threatened to leap from her chest as the limo pulled up in front of the building. There was a line of other limos, with photographers and reporters lining the entrance. She didn't belong here. She belonged back at the manor, watching a movie with the boys.

There was only one car ahead of hers, and she thought she might faint. Why the hell had she agreed to go to the gala with Jonathan? Why hadn't she turned him down? This was so far out of her comfort zone.

And yet here she was, in a dress that cost more than she'd ever seen in her lifetime, wearing jewelry that probably could've paid for the rest of her college expenses. She didn't even look like herself, with her hair and make-up done to perfection. She hadn't wanted to embarrass Jonathan, so she'd made sure everything was perfect before they'd left the house.

But that wouldn't do any good if she passed out the moment the stepped out of the car. She could just see a picture of herself in a crumpled heap on the front page of the paper tomorrow. She'd never be able to live that one down.

It didn't help that she still hadn't told him about the baby. After he'd invited her to the gala, the words had gotten stuck in her throat. She wanted them to have at least one nice night together before she broke the news and risked everything.

After tonight, she decided, she'd sit down and tell him.

When Jonathan reached over and took hold of her hand, she turned to see him smiling at her. He squeezed her hand gently. "Take a deep breath. Everything will be okay, I promise."

Trisha nodded, giving him a shaky smile. She wanted to believe him, but her body was in full revolt right then. Nothing short of popping a few Xanax was going to help her calm down right now. And with her being pregnant, that was out of the question.

Finally, it was there turn. The chauffer stopped the car, then walked around to open the door. Jonathan slid out first, then offered his hand to Trisha.

*It's now or never*, she told herself. She took a deep breath, then grasped Jonathan's hand and let him help her from the car. Immediately, she was assaulted by the blinding flashes of a thousand cameras going off at once.

She tried to smile as Jonathan slipped his arm around her waist and let her up the walkway. Her knees wobbled as she walked, but at least she didn't topple over. Thank god for small favors, right?

Once they were through the doors and her eyes were able to adjust, she felt much better. At least she'd made it through that little gauntlet. She had no idea how celebrities dealt with that kind of attention all the time.

It was insane!

Jonathan seemed to know exactly where he was going, so she let him lead the way. Soon, they were in a massive ballroom with people milling around. Everyone in there was dressed to the nines. She had a feeling every outfit, even those on the servers wandering about, cost way more than she'd ever be able to afford.

Once again, she wondered why she was here. Then she'd catch Jonathan's eye and he'd smile at her and she'd remember. She couldn't say no to him. When he'd shown her that dress and the necklace he'd bought, she wanted to melt into the floor.

He could've asked her to lead a mission to Mars and she'd have agreed to it.

As soon as they walked into the room, people started coming over to shake Jonathan's hand. He introduced her to each person, but most of the names went in one ear and out the other. It was a wonder he was able to remember every single person. There was no way she would be able to.

A server approached and offered them each glasses of champagne. Jonathan took one, then looked at her curiously when she declined. Some alcohol would've gone a long way to helping her calm her nerves, but she wasn't going to risk it.

Then a man and a woman walked over and Jonathan grinned. He embraced the man, the two of them patting each other on the back. Then he turned to the woman, dressed in a light blew gown, with curly blonde hair and a beautiful sapphire necklace. He took her hand, lifted it to his lips, and kissed it. He reminded Trisha of a prince out of a fairy tale.

She giggled, then smacked him gently on the arm, shaking her head. "That's enough of that, you!"

Jonathan nodded. Then, he slipped his arm around Trisha's waist again and pushed her forward slightly. "Trisha, I'd like to introduce you to Timothy. He's my best friend and the man in charge or R&D at AshCorp. And this is his wife, Sarah,"

"It's a pleasure to meet you," she said, forcing a smile onto her face and shaking Timothy's hand. Then the woman gave her a polite hug.

"It's a great to meet you," Timothy said. "Jonathan has told me so much about you."

Trisha looked at the floor. Jonathan had talked about her to other people? She could only imagine what he'd said…

Sarah walked to stand next to her, putting a hand on her shoulder. "Don't worry, it's all been good stuff. Now how about I introduce you to the other women here? We'll let the men mingle and do their thing."

When Jonathan smiled at her, Trisha nodded. She let

Sarah lead her away, her heart pounding as she did so. She'd expected to stay glued to Jonathan's side the entire night, not being forced to interact with woman she'd never met before.

Sarah was friendly enough, though she still felt awkward meeting all the different women. These were all women who were completely different from here. They'd all grown up with silver spoons in their mouths, not having to work their asses off for every scrap they got.

But every once in a while, she'd look across the room and see Jonathan smiling at her and her heart would flutter. As long as he was here, she could do this. She wasn't going to let a bunch of high society women get the better of her.

She was starting to get more comfortable until Sarah excused herself to use the ladies' room, leaving Trisha with three women she'd barely even met. They reminded her of a high school clique. Debra was a tall, shrew looking woman who seemed to be their little ring leader.

"Looks like the press it eating up whatever Mr. Ashcourt is feeding them over there." Debra looked passed Trisha to where Jonathan stood talking with a reporter. Then the woman sneered at Trisha. "I'm surprised he doesn't have you over there on his arm, looking all pretty for them."

Trisha blinked, then furrowed her brow. "Why would he want me to be with him?"

Debra snickered and her little friends did the same. Trisha frowned now. Obviously there was some kind of inside joke that she wasn't privy to.

"Look honey, it's nice that you get to live out your little Cinderella fantasy here, but at midnight, that carriage is going to turn back into a pumpkin." Debra smirked at Trisha. "We all know why you're really here. You're nothing but a prop so Mr. Ashcourt can have some positive press in the news tomorrow. You're a distraction so nobody thinks about why he's really opening up this hospital."

Trisha's hands balled into fists. Anger flooded through her body at her insinuation. Was that what they all thought? That she's just a publicity stunt to help him look better for the press? "He's doing it for the kids! For everyone who still lives down in those projects! He brought me along because he wanted me to be here, not as some kind of arm candy."

Debra laughed openly, her friends still snickering,

which just made Trisha angrier. It took all of her willpower not to just deck the woman. How anyone had married such a shrew, Trisha would never know.

"Oh honey, you're so naive. Have you even asked him what his company's plans are? They've been buying up land in a twenty block radius of that hospital. The projects will be ancient history in a few years." She grinned broader now. "We're talking condos, high rise luxury apartments. All of those poor, poor people will be out of their homes soon enough."

She faked a frown as she spoke, then smiled again. It was obvious she didn't care about anyone but herself. But Jonathan wasn't like that. He wouldn't toss people out of their homes just to make a quick buck. "You're wrong!"

"I'm never wrong... My husband is the lead architect of the redevelopment project. Investors aren't going to fund building a state of the art hospital in the middle of a rundown area. It's just not a good investment."

Again, there was that high pitched giggle that grated on Trisha's nerves. She wanted to rip the champagne glass out of the woman's hands and smash it over her head.

"Clearly you're above your depth here. I don't know

what will be bigger news, the fact that he is opening up this hospital and rebuilding downtown, or the fact that he's dating someone so far outside his *circle*..."

"What the hell is that supposed to mean?" Trisha's nails dug into her palms as she fought to control herself. She'd never felt like this before, never felt this much anger coursing through her veins.

Debra smirked and the other two girls giggled. "Oh *honey*, you know *exactly* what I mean." Her eyes looked up and down Trisha's body, her thoughts clearly visible. Trisha was nothing more than a publicity tool in her eyes, something to be used and discarded afterwards.

Trisha's anger began to bubble over now. But instead of punching the woman in the face, she turned and stalked out of the room, not once looking back. How fucking dare she insult Trisha like that. Worse, how dare she say those things about Jonathan.

But hadn't Trisha had those same thoughts herself? She *was* so far outside Jonathan's social circle she was surprised she even registered on his radar. She didn't grow up rich. She didn't grow up going to private schools and having her schooling paid for without a second thought.

She slipped out a side door, avoiding anyone who might still be out front, then she sat down on the curb, pulling her knees up against her chest. She completely ignored the people walking along behind her, completely lost in her own mind.

Her parents had worked their asses off to get out of the projects. And she'd worked her ass off to go to school, to get accepted into one of the most prestigious universities in the state. She'd worked her ass off to get as many scholarships as possible.

To hear someone talk about the projects like that…

She still had friends and family there. Shew knew plenty of people who busted their asses just to keep food on the table and the electricity turned on. These were people who couldn't afford to buy a house of their own and were dependent on landlords who barely maintained their buildings.

What if what Debra had said was true? What if Jonathan's company really was buying up all the land around the hospital? Where would everyone that lived there go? There was no way they could afford to pack up and move somewhere else.

Her hands went to her stomach as she thought about the baby growing inside her. God, how could she have a kid with a man who'd toss people out of their homes just to make the area more appealing to investors?

Worse, how could she have a kid with a man who just wanted to show up with her on his arm for the media? Trisha, the poor black girl who'd barely escaped the projects. Boy, wouldn't that make some headlines in the morning.

Her anger once again surfacing, she stood and hailed a cab. She needed to get out of here. Needed to get away from Jonathan, at least until she had time to think. And she wasn't going to get much thinking done sitting on the curb in front of the AshCorp gala.

Once in the cab, she gave him this address, hoping Samantha would be home. Sure enough, when she knocked on the door, Samantha opened it a few moments later, dressed in her pajamas and a pint of ice cream in her hands.

Sam smirked, then stepped aside to let Trisha inside. "Well don't I feel underdressed now."

"Can I borrow an extra set of PJs? I need somewhere to crash for the night."

"Uh oh, that doesn't sound good. I think I'm going to need some more ice cream."

A few minutes later and Trisha was dressed in a pair of Sam's pajamas, the two of them sitting on the couch, each with a pint of ice cream in their hands. Trisha wished she could have a glass of wine or something to help settle her nerves, but she couldn't risk it with the baby.

"Oh, you don't really believe that rich snob, do you?" Sam rolled her eyes. "Has he ever done anything that would make you think you were just a publicity stunt? I thought you liked him."

"I *do* like him. But he hasn't exactly been open about our relationship. It wasn't until I'd confronted him that he'd asked me to go to the gala with him. What if the only reason he took me was so that he could show me off to all those reporters? Maybe it had just been sex until he realized he could use me for more than that."

Trisha closed her eyes and fought back the tears that formed. She didn't want to believe any of this, didn't even want to consider it. But now that the seed had been planted, that was all she could think of. What would happen when Jonathan found out she was pregnant?

The image of him dragging her to an abortion clinic flashed in front of her mind, making her shudder.

There was no way she was giving up this kid. She wasn't keen on trying to raise a kid alone, but that's what she'd do if she needed to.

"Did you try talking to him?" Sam asked.

Trisha shook her head. "No. I just left before I punched that woman. And I turned off my phone on the way here. I wasn't in the mood to hear any of his excuses."

"Trisha… If you don't talk to him, how are you going to find out the truth? You can't let what that woman said get to you. You need to sit down and talk to him. You have to tell him about the baby."

"Switch," Trisha said, trading pints of ice cream with Sam. "But what if everything she said is true? What if he really is going to tear down the projects and build a bunch of condos or something? How am I supposed to raise a kid with a guy like that?"

Sam nudged her. "You don't really think he'd do that, do you?"

Wasn't that the billion-dollar question?

No, she didn't want to believe he'd do something like that. She wanted him to be a good man. But was that the reality or was that just her heart talking? Was he really a good person or did she just want to believe that because she was falling in love with him?

He was a good father, she admitted to herself. Even if he did practically live at work, he never ignored the boys. He rarely yelled at them. And he'd never raised a hand to them. They both clearly adored their father and loved him more than anything.

But those were his sons. Would he feel the same compassion for people he'd never met? People who might not have even registered on his radar? Or were they below him, below caring about?

"I don't know," Trisha said, honestly. "I just don't know what to think."

Sam set her ice cream on the coffee table, then put her arm around Trisha. Trisha leaned into her friend, glad she's decided to come here. Sam had always been by her side, was the one rock she could always return to, no matter what.

"Sleep on it then. You can crash on the couch tonight; this way you don't have to see him until tomorrow. Maybe then you'll know what you think. And then you can talk to him and decide where to go from there, okay?"

Trisha nodded. It sounded like a better plan than anything else she'd come up with. Part of her never wanted to see Jonathan again. But another part of her needed to hear the truth from him. Needed to hear that those women were wrong, about his plans for the projects and for her.

## 24

### JONATHAN

Jonathan had slept fitfully all night, wondering where Trisha was. He'd called her phone dozens of times, but his calls had gone straight to her voicemail. Why the hell had she left the gala without telling him? Had he done something wrong?

He knew she'd been a bit awkward being surrounded by all those people, but he'd thought she was adjusting as she'd gotten to know Sarah. Besides, he was right across the room if she'd needed him. So why had she run off so abruptly without even saying something to him?

By the time the sun had risen, he'd barely gotten any sleep. Finally, he kicked off the covers and hopped in the shower. This time though, the hot water did nothing to ease his nerves. He was just as restless when he stepped out as when he'd gotten in.

The only difference was some of the fatigue had faded slightly. Now his mind worked in overdrive, various scenarios going through his head all at once. Each image that flashed before his eyes was worse than the last.

He ended up pacing around the house, trying to figure out what to do. Should he call the cops and report her missing? He doubted they'd take him all that seriously, probably just laugh and tell him he'd been dumped.

But he couldn't believe that.

Trisha wasn't the type of woman to just dump a guy for no reason. And he was pretty sure she wasn't the type to not even tell a guy things were over. When she'd tried to end things last time, at least she'd told him up front about how she felt.

Jonathan froze, staring at the window. Had she changed her mind about not wanting to break up with him?

She'd said she wanted to break up with him before, but that was when their relationship was nothing but sex. Last night was supposed to be their first official date together, their first outing as more than just a man and his nanny.

Had she decided he wasn't worth dating?

He was thankful the boys were still with their friends. At least they didn't need to see him having a mental breakdown as he wracked his brain, trying to figure out what had gone wrong. What was he going to tell them if he picked them up and Trisha still hadn't come home?

Declan would be crushed if he never got to see her again. He was pretty sure even Alexander wouldn't be happy, even if he wasn't thrilled with the thought of them dating. So how was he supposed to explain things to them, when he didn't even know what was going on himself?

Thankfully, Trisha showed up around nine that morning, being dropped off by a taxi. He practically ran to the front door just as Trisha was walking inside. She wore a t-shirt and jeans and had a small bag with what looked like her dress and necklace in it.

Jonathan's mouth went dry as he stared at her, trying to figure out what he should say.

"We need to talk," she said, breaking the silence. Those

simple words nearly made his heart stop beating all together. "Are the boys home?"

He shook his head. "No. They're still at their friends'."

"Good," Trisha said with a nod. "Can we go somewhere and sit?"

Jonathan studied her face for a moment. She wore no make-up today, and her cheeks were tear stained. This didn't seem like it was going to be a good chat. He wanted to pull her into his arms and tell her everything would be okay. But he doubted that would be the best course of action.

Instead, he nodded and lead her to the sitting room. The last time they'd sat together in there was when Jonathan had been interviewing her for the positon. In a way, their relationship had begun in this room. He hoped he wasn't about to end in this room, too.

Trisha sat in one of the chairs and Jonathan sat across from her. She looked down at her lap, her hands clenched into fists. It looked like she was fighting back tears again. What was going through her head?

When she didn't speak, Jonathan did. "What's going on, Trisha? What happened last night? Where did you go?"

"I… I went back to my old apartment. I stayed with Sam for the night."

Trisha kept her eyes downcast. Her left leg bounced up and down, as if she could barely contain her nerves. She had the look of a girl who'd just had a glimpse into Hell and had no idea what to do. That just made Jonathan even more scared.

"Is everything okay with her? She's not sick or anything, is she?" He fought the urge to stand up and pace around the room. His body was practically shaking. He couldn't ever remember feeling anxiousness or nerves like this before. Not even when he had to stand in front of crowds of people and cameras for press conferences.

Trisha shook her head. She brushed a hand across her eyes. "No, she's fine. I just…. I needed time to think."

"To think about what?"

"About us…"

Jonathan could barely hear anything over his heart beating. His worst fears seemed to be coming true. Trisha had changed her mind and didn't want anything to do with him. Just when he'd thought he'd finally found someone, she wanted nothing to do with him.

Wasn't that just his luck?

Now his mouth and throat were even drier than before. He considered going to grab himself some whiskey to help calm his nerves, but it wasn't even noon yet.

"What do you mean?" he asked.

Trisha stood abruptly and began pacing around the room. Once again, Jonathan had to fight back the urge to pull her into his arms. His own hands balled into fists as he struggled to come up with something he could do or say to help put her at ease.

Neither of them spoke for a minute or two. Jonathan just watched Trisha pace, waiting for her to give him something he could work with. Something that would tell him what was going on inside her head.

"Is it true you're buying up all the land around where the new hospital is being built?" She asked as she stared out the window, her arms crossed in front of her chest.

Jonathan blinked. What the heck was she talking about? Why the sudden change of topics?

"Yes, we are. Why? What does that have to do with anything?"

Trisha whirled around. She glared at him now, her

hands in tight fists. It looked like she was about to attack him. What the heck had gotten into her?

"How could you do that?" She yelled. "People live there! Good people…. I have friends… and family… that live down there. I can't believe you'd do that!"

"What are you talking about?" Jonathan stood and walked over to her. He tried to pull her into his arms, but she yanked away from him. "Trisha, will you just tell me what's going on?"

"I can't believe you. I thought you were better than that." She brushed tears from her eyes, though they came right back. "I can't believe you'd throw people out of their homes just to build pretty little condos. I never thought you'd be so selfish and greedy."

Now Jonathan was really confused. Why did she think he was planning to build condos around the hospital? Hell, how had she known he was buying up the land around there? The only people who knew anything about the project were supposed to be those working on it.

"Come with me." Jonathan took her hand and lead her up to his study. Even though she tried to pull away, he kept firm. She needed to know the truth, and he wasn't going to let her run away without hearing all of it."

Once inside the office, he picked up his briefcase and pulled out a bunch of files, laying them out on his desk. As he did so, he spoke to her. "My company has been planning this hospital for years now. It will be the first 'smart' hospital. The first of many, we hope. Everything will be connected and managed through our MediPads.

"Everything from patient charts to x-rays and CAT scans can be viewed on the devices. The doctors can use it to write prescriptions, to monitor their patients' vitals, hell they can even order their lunch from the cafeteria. Everything in the hospital will be connected."

"That sounds cool, but what does that have to do with anything?" Trisha had her hands on her hips, glaring at him again. Apparently she wasn't all that impressed with his plans.

"I'm getting to that." He rolled his eyes. "We started buying up the land around the hospital last year. We'd gotten the land for the hospital dirt cheap because no businesses wanted to open in that part of town. When we started doing more digging, we found out about the horrible conditions of the area.

"Most of the houses and apartment complexes are falling apart. Even the landlords don't care about maintaining their property. Most of the land is up for sale and for pennies on the dollar at that. After that, I started talking to the other executives and we started making plans."

Jonathan waved his hands at the papers spread out in front of them. They were all architectural designs. He'd had the architects that had designed the hospital do these up, though they were still in the working stages and weren't complete.

"We designed a bunch of low cost, easy to maintain apartment complexes. We've been buying the land to rejuvenate it, to bring life back to the area. What good is having a state of the art hospital if the people who need it most can't even live in a house that's not falling down around them? We're not trying to throw them out or build 'pretty little condos'. We're trying to *help* people."

Trisha stared openly at him, her mouth hanging open as she did so. Then she crossed the room to look at the papers spread out on his desk. She picked them up, one at a time, carefully studying each one of them. She didn't speak until she'd looked over every single one of the papers.

"You're... you mean you're not building condos and

high rises? You're not trying to gentrify the area to make your hospital look better? So you can make even more money off everything?"

Jonathan shook his head, frowning. "No! Where did you get that idea from? Sure, the MediPads and our Smart Hospital will bring in a lot of money for the company, but it'll help even more people. The more simple processes are automated, the more time the doctors and nurses can spend actually working with their patients.

"The new apartments and houses will give the people living down in the projects a better shot at life. They'll be safer, so they can focus on other things, instead of wondering when the walls will fall down around them. Everything will be cleaner, safer, and help keep them from needing the hospital."

Jonathan moved from behind his desk to stand in front of Trisha. He took her hands in his and kissed them before looking into her eyes.

"I'm not some kind of selfish bastard. I wouldn't dream of just tossing people out on the streets to make a quick buck. That's what last night's gala was about. I've been working to raise money to help subsidize the costs of building everything, so the places can be even more affordable for the people living there."

Trisha closed her eyes. She didn't try to pull away from him this time. Nor did she try to wipe away the tears the slid down her cheeks. Jonathan waited for her to speak, waited for her to let him know what was going on in her head now.

"I'm… I'm sorry." Trisha's cheeks were bright pink now. "I had no idea. When I heard about you buying up all the land… I shouldn't have doubted you. I'm sorry."

When Trisha tried to walked away, Jonathan kept a firm grip on her hands. He wasn't about to let her run away. Not this time. She's slipped through his fingers last night, but he wasn't about to let her out of his sight now.

"You don't have to be sorry." Jonathan pulled her into his arms, wrapping his arms firmly around her waist. "I wish you'd just come to me last night. That's why you ran out on the gala, isn't it?"

Trisha nodded. "It was stupid. I shouldn't have listened to anything that vile woman said."

"What else did she say?" he dreaded her answer, but

needed to know. He needed to know what else was bothering her.

"She said you only brought me to the gala to show me off for the media. The pretty little black girl on your arm so no one would question you destroying the projects." She wiped away another tear that had threatened to escape.

"I brought you to the gala because I wanted everyone to see the wonderful woman I'd met. Just like you, I was tired of things just being sex between us. I wanted more." He shook his head. "No, I needed more. I need you here, in my arms, forever."

"You mean that?" She looked at up at him, her chocolate eyes shimmering.

He nodded, then leaned down and kissed her gently. Sparks danced between them for that brief moment. "I… I love you, Trisha."

Trisha opened her mouth to say something, then closed it. She looked into his eyes for a few moments, then leaned against his chest and cried. Jonathan held her tight until her crying subsided.

"What's wrong?" he asked, worried. Did she not feel the same way about him?

"There's something I need to tell you." She sniffled. When she pulled away from him and turned around, Jonathan waked up and wrapped her arms around her waist again, pulling her back against his chest.

"You can tell me anything."

"I'm pregnant."

Jonathan froze. The two simple words seemed to have made his brain completely shut down. Pregnant? As far as he knew, he'd been the only one that she'd slept with recently. And they hadn't even thought to use condoms or anything.

That meant...

"Is it... Is it mine?" he asked, his mouth dry again. When Trisha nodded, Jonathan tried to swallow the lump in his throat.

Pregnant. Trisha was pregnant. With his child.

He was going to be a father, again.

His heart hammered now, faster than it had in years. They were going to have a baby! Trisha and him were going to have a baby!

He turned Trisha around, then pressed their lips firmly

together. "I love you so much," he said, breaking the kiss. "When should we tell the boys?"

"You're… you're not mad?"

Jonathan shook his head. "How could I be mad? I wish you'd told me sooner, but no, I'm not mad. It'll be strange to have a baby in the house again, but there's no one else I'd rather have a child with. I told you, Trisha, I love you."

"I love you, too," she said at last, making his entire being swell. "I've waited so long to say those words to you."

Jonathan grinned at her, unable to fight the happiness welling up inside him. Another kid hadn't even been on his list of things to do, but he couldn't deny being excited. Part of him missed having a little guy running around the house, now that the boys were growing up.

He couldn't wait to have another son or even his first daughter. And he couldn't think of anyone better to raise a kid with than Trisha.

"You know this means I'll have to hire a new nanny, right?"

Trisha's eyes went wide, her face pale. "What? Why?"

"Because…." Jonathan kissed her on the nose. "If my wife is busy taking care of a baby, someone has to help with the other two. You think they're a handful now, just wait until you have and infant to deal with. Plus, you still have school."

Trisha buried her head in his chest. She shook in his arms as he felt tear soak into his shirt. He held her tighter, vowing to never let go. He'd never find a woman like this again, and he knew that. Now he just needed to make sure this one didn't go anywhere.

When Trisha's tears subsided, Jonathan gently lifted her head until they looked deep into each other's eyes. He leaned forward and kissed her again. "How about we go to the bedroom and celebrate before we have to go pick up the boys?"

Trisha flushed scarlet, but she nodded, a small smile appearing. Then, after a moment, her smile turned into a wicked smirk. "I think I know just the way to celebrate!"

Jonathan was still grinning like a fool as she led him from the room. It didn't get much better than this, he thought to himself. He was looking forward to spending the rest of his life with Trisha, starting with tonight!

## 25

### TRISHA

The grin on Trisha's face seemed to be permanent. Today was the day Jonathan had been looking forward to for years. This was the day where his dream would finally come true. And standing on the stage behind him, Trisha couldn't have been prouder.

Alexander and Declan stood next to her, both dressed in their nicest clothes and grinning just as broadly as she was. They both knew how much today meant to their father. They'd been talking nonstop, both apparently excited to be on TV, even if it was just them standing behind their father.

*Boys*, Trisha thought as she shook her head. Then she looked over at little Justin and her heart swelled. The tiny four-year-old was on her hips, his eyes wide as he looked around at the crowd. His milk-chocolate skin was a stark contract to the pale white of Alexander and Declan, but there was no denying they were related.

All three had the same inquisitive eyes and energetic nature. No one who say the three of them together would even be able to think they were anything but brothers. If Justin hadn't had her eyes and skin color, he'd have been their tiny twin.

Declan in particular had really taken to the role of Big Brother. In fact, he'd been the one who'd wanted to hold Justin today. If Declan had his way, he'd carry his baby brother everywhere.

When they'd first told the boys about Trisha being pregnant, Declan had started bouncing off the walls, going over everything he wanted to teach his little sibling. And now that Justin was finally getting old enough to learn a few things, Declan had appointed himself Justin's mentor.

Trisha and Jonathan had sat on lawn chairs, watching as Declan taught Justin how to ride a tricycle, with Alexander watching the two of them like a hawk, helping when needed.

Alexander hadn't been thrilled with Trisha becoming a permanent part of their family, but he'd adjusted.

Jonathan had talked to Alexander a few times, letting him know Trisha wasn't there to replace the boys' mother.

After that, he'd opened up and gone back to normal.

The four, and then five, of them had become a family. Jonathan did his best to be home for dinner each night. He'd even taken the boys on weekend trips fairly often, spending a lot more time with the two of them than he had before. And, once the baby was born, he'd hired a new nanny to help take some of the burden off of Trisha so she could focus on finishing school and taking care of the baby.

Trish had finished out her undergrad degree without issues. Jonathan and the boys had all been there at her graduation ceremony, cheering as she'd walked across the stage. The only time she'd ever felt happier was on her wedding day, with all of her friends and family in attendance. But hearing everyone yelling her name as she received her diploma had made her grin like a fool.

He'd supported her through her Master's program, always being there when she need a shoulder to lean on. He'd even offered her a job working in the new hospital after she graduated, but she'd turned him down, not quite ready for that yet. Instead, she was working with a small, local practice now, helping counsel abused children.

One day, she might take Jonathan up on the offer to work with the hospital, but not yet. She wanted to be confident in her skills and knowledge before she took on a project that big. But it would be her new goal, working through the hospital to help the children who came through its doors.

But right now, it was Jonathan's turn to have everyone here for him. Trisha and the boys were behind him, along with some of the other executives from AshCorp, but the rest of Jonathan's friends and family were out in the audience. Even Gretta and her husband, as well as Judith, were out there to support him.

"Today is a historic day," Jonathan said, making the crowd go silent. "Today we open AshCorp Hospital, the next step in medical advancement. This hospital and everything inside it has a been a dream of mine, and many of those at AshCorp, for many years now.

"With the latest advancements in medical technology, we're bringing top of the line healthcare to those who need it most. Now, healthcare can be easier, quicker, and more affordable for everyone. Why should the best care be limited to just those who can afford it?

"We've spent years building the hospital. Now, to see it standing behind me in all its glory, it's like seeing my dream in person for the first time. Together with our low cost housing, AshCorp will revitalize the city, finally giving the poor a chance to move up in life."

When Jonathan paused, the crowd burst out in applause. There were cameras everywhere, all running constantly, focused on Jonathan. If Trisha had been up in his place, she'd have been shaking with nerves. But despite all the attention, Jonathan didn't seem to be phased in the least.

Trisha wanted to run up and wrap her arms around him for comfort, but she stood firm behind him. Instead, she put her arm around Declan's shoulders. He looked up at her and grinned, and the butterflies in her stomach settled.

As she focused on the boys standing on either side of her, and Jonathan standing in front, her entire body seemed to relax. She could do this, she told herself. She could stand here and support her husband. She wasn't the same woman she was four years ago.

But when Jonathan looked over his shoulder, locked eyes with her, and smiled, a different kind of butterflies filled her stomach. No matter how long they'd been together, no matter how many nights they'd spent in each other's arms, Jonathan never ceased to make her heart pound its hardest.

"I've had a fortunate life. I have a wonderful family, with all the opportunities of the world at my fingertips. I know a lot of people don't have the options I do. Which is why all of this is so important to me. Everyone deserves a shot at success, at happiness. Even those born into poverty deserve healthcare and housing they can afford.

"It is my hope, that the people of this city will be able to work their way out of poverty, now that they don't have to worry about their houses falling apart or a broken bone being a debt sentence. It is my hope that the future generations of the people living in the projects will have more opportunities available to them, that there will be nothing they can't do."

Trisha grinned broadly now. Not only had Jonathan used AshCorp funds and investors to fund all of this, but he'd sunk quite a bit of his own money into these projects. He really did care about those around him, even if he didn't even know them.

She couldn't believe she'd ever doubted him. That was the last time she'd ever listened to the opinion of a woman she'd never even met before. She should've known better than to believe a single thing that woman had said. She'd been the type of woman Trisha despised above all others, yet she'd listened to everything that shrew had said and let it get to her.

Never again, she vowed. She would stand behind Jonathan no matter what happened. She would stand beside Alexander, Declan, and Justin for the rest of her life. Just like she knew they'd be there for her, she would be there for all of them.

Her family.

Made in the USA
Columbia, SC
28 December 2019